"My, what big ... Sarah whisper...

She knew she was playing a dangerous game, but she couldn't seem to stop herself. No, she didn't *want* to stop herself.

"All the better to hold you with," Michael said, taking her mouth in a hungry kiss, before pulling her body flush with his own. Sensations overwhelmed Sarah. Cool against hot. Soft against hard. The intimate contact made her long for more, made her forget everything but this man. This moment.

As his mouth devoured her, his fingers stalked the buttons of her blouse, the zipper on her skirt. Before she knew it, she was wearing nothing but her lacy red bra and panties, lingerie bought on a whim yesterday to implement her New Year's resolution to take more risks. No more boring beige underwear.

No more boring beige life.

"And what big hands you have," she gasped as his touches became more intimate.

She could sense rather than see his predatory smile.

"All the better to ravish you with, my dear."

Dear Reader,

My New Year's resolutions are usually fairly tame: lose weight, become more organized, stop procrastinating. Resolutions I usually manage to break before Valentine's Day, unlike my heroine, Sarah Hewitt, who makes a New Year's resolution to take more risks—a resolution that ultimately lands her in the bed of Michael Wolff, a sexy stranger who's determined not to let her go…literally. Now all Sarah has to decide is *if* she wants to escape!

I had so much fun writing a story for THE WRONG BED, one of Temptation's most popular miniseries. And I'd love to know what you think about Michael and Sarah's story. You can reach me online at www.KristinGabriel.com or write to me at P.O. Box 5162, Grand Island, Nebraska 68801-5162.

Enjoy!

Kristin Gabriel

Books by Kristin Gabriel

HARLEQUIN TEMPTATION
834—DANGEROUSLY IRRESISTIBLE
868—SEDUCED IN SEATTLE
896—SHEERLY IRRESISTIBLE

HARLEQUIN DUETS
7—ANNIE, GET YOUR GROOM
25—THE BACHELOR TRAP
27—BACHELOR BY DESIGN
29—BEAUTY AND THE BACHELOR
61—OPERATION BABE-MAGNET
OPERATION BEAUTY

CS

Propositioned?
Kristin Gabriel

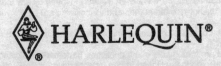

HARLEQUIN®

TORONTO • NEW YORK • LONDON
AMSTERDAM • PARIS • SYDNEY • HAMBURG
STOCKHOLM • ATHENS • TOKYO • MILAN • MADRID
PRAGUE • WARSAW • BUDAPEST • AUCKLAND

This book is dedicated to my readers.
I hope wonderful things await you in the New Year!

ISBN 0-373-69109-2

PROPOSITIONED?

Copyright © 2003 by Kristin Eckhardt.

All rights reserved. Except for use in any review, the reproduction or
utilization of this work in whole or in part in any form by any electronic,
mechanical or other means, now known or hereafter invented, including
xerography, photocopying and recording, or in any information storage
or retrieval system, is forbidden without the written permission of the
publisher, Harlequin Enterprises Limited, 225 Duncan Mill Road,
Don Mills, Ontario, Canada M3B 3K9.

All characters in this book have no existence outside the imagination of
the author and have no relation whatsoever to anyone bearing the same
name or names. They are not even distantly inspired by any individual
known or unknown to the author, and all incidents are pure invention.

This edition published by arrangement with Harlequin Books S.A.

® and TM are trademarks of the publisher. Trademarks indicated with
® are registered in the United States Patent and Trademark Office, the
Canadian Trade Marks Office and in other countries.

Visit us at www.eHarlequin.com

Printed in U.S.A.

1

SARAH HEWITT had never crashed a party before. Or broken into a safe. But there was a first time for everything, and tonight she was planning to do both.

Her black leather boots crunched in the snow as she stealthily approached the Wolff mansion. Bright lights shone from the tall windows gracing the front of the grand edifice, casting an eerie crystal glow on the snowy mountainside. Towering pine trees surrounded the open black wrought-iron gate, making it easy for her to slip inside the private grounds unnoticed.

She'd left her twelve-year-old Toyota parked on an unpaved road a half mile away. The crisp mountain air had numbed her cheeks as she'd made the remainder of the journey to the Wolff mansion on foot. Now her breath came in quick, uneven puffs of frosty air, though more from the anticipation of the night ahead than the steep uphill hike she'd just taken. Adrenaline pumped through her veins now, warming her from the inside out. She wiggled her frozen toes inside her boots as sharp pinpricks of feeling slowly flowed back into them.

From her vantage point on the mountain, she could see tiny dots of lights marking the city of Denver, which lay twenty miles to the east. That's where she lived with her grandfather, who assumed Sarah was out celebrating New Year's Eve with her friends.

Little did he know she was about to follow his footsteps into a life of crime.

She moved swiftly in the shadows toward the mansion, watching as a steady string of shiny black limousines made their way around the circular driveway. Each one stopped briefly at the front entrance to let its costumed passengers disembark.

The Wolffs' annual masquerade ball was one of the highlights of the Denver social season. Or so she'd heard. Sarah didn't pay much attention to lives of the rich and famous. She was too busy trying to earn enough money so she could finally pursue her master's degree in sociology. She was currently working two jobs—as a bank teller during the day and a waitress evenings and weekends.

When Sarah had glimpsed an invitation to the Wolffs' masquerade ball on the bank president's desk, she knew it had been a little nudge from fate. It couldn't have simply been by chance that she'd been given the perfect opportunity to correct a horrible mistake before it came back to haunt her family.

Standing near the front entrance now, hidden behind a massive marble column, Sarah watched as the doorman stood inside the open foyer to welcome the arriving guests. She pulled her long, hooded red cloak more tightly around her, grateful she'd picked a warm costume.

Little Red Riding Hood's red wool cloak, elbow-length red gloves, and black leather boots were perfect for traipsing around a mountain in the middle of winter. As an added advantage, the gloves would ensure that she left no telltale fingerprints behind.

Peering through the slits of her red mask, she leaned farther around the column to see a commotion in the foyer. One of the arriving guests, a woman dressed as a Las Vegas showgirl, had gotten her tall feather headdress stuck on the crystal chandelier.

As the doorman struggled to untangle the distraught showgirl, Sarah quickly raced up the steps and moved inside the foyer, heading rapidly for the ballroom. The loud band music reverberating down the hallway would have led her there, even if she hadn't memorized the blueprint of the mansion's floor plans the night before.

Sarah held her breath as she hurried down the hallway, half-expecting someone to sound an alarm and cut her off before she could lose herself among the crowd of costumed guests milling around the opulent ballroom. But to her surprise, no one tried to stop her. She soon found herself standing at the arched doorway to the ballroom, mercifully anony-mous behind her mask.

Relief washed over her, though she knew the greater challenge lay ahead. She let her gaze wander over the ballroom, impressed with the polished mar-ble floor and the crystal chandeliers hanging from the vaulted ceiling. All of the guests wore masks to conceal their identity. According to the party invita-tion, the grand unveiling was scheduled for mid-night.

That's when Sarah intended to make her move.

She checked her watch, realizing she'd allowed herself plenty of time. Now she simply had to blend in and mingle for the next hour or so, try to act as if she really belonged here. Sarah couldn't wait until this night was over. Then she could return to her reg-ular life. In a regular house. With regular people.

If she didn't land herself in prison first.

She sucked a deep breath of air at that thought and tightened her grip on the small wicker picnic basket she carried in the crook of her arm. It wasn't as if she'd come here tonight to actually *steal* anything. Just the opposite, in fact. Sarah was here for the ex-press purpose of returning the diamond necklace presently inside her basket to the safe on the third floor of the Wolff mansion, where it belonged.

And she desperately needed to do it before anyone noticed the necklace was missing. Before they could accuse her grandfather, Bertram Hewitt, of stealing it. Again.

Unfortunately, her grandfather was guilty, though he truly believed it was no more than he deserved. Forty years ago, Bertram Hewitt and Seamus Wolff had gone into the estate business together, purchasing entire households of possessions belonging to the recently deceased, then reselling them at a profit. After only two prosperous years, Seamus Wolff had abruptly demanded they close their business and split all the assets in half.

Bertram claimed to this day that Seamus knew about the diamond necklace stashed in one of the old trunks—a trunk Seamus had made certain he received as his part of the business settlement. The man had gone on to become a multimillionaire, using the valuable necklace as collateral to embark on several very successful business ventures. Meanwhile, Bertram had eked out a living in a pawnshop, certain that he'd been cheated by his old friend.

So he'd stolen it with the best of intentions, determined to provide Sarah with her rightful legacy. Not that the police would care. They certainly hadn't cared eighteen years ago when he'd stolen the necklace the first time, hoping to save his dying wife.

Her grandfather's bitterness had only grown deeper in prison. He'd vowed to get the necklace back again. And he'd done just that two weeks ago, blending in among a crew of house painters while the Wolff family was in Jamaica over Christmas.

Fortunately, they hadn't noticed the necklace missing yet, or the police would be at their door once more. That's why Sarah had to return it now, while there was still a chance to save her grandfather.

"Do you have something in that basket for me?" The deep voice curled around her spine.

Sarah's heart thumped wildly in her chest as she slowly turned around to see a man-size wolf hovering over her. The shirt and pants of his costume were made of thick, black fur, so plush over his broad chest she had to resist the urge to reach out and stroke it.

"Nothing that would interest you," she lied. "You might try the buffet table."

Even if she hadn't recognized his voice, she'd know those eyes anywhere. Michael Wolff. Ruthless businessman and notorious playboy. Grandson of Seamus Wolff. Natural enemy of the Hewitts.

Did he recognize her? She worked at the bank in the building he owned, but he'd never been one of her customers. Besides, her costume concealed her almost from head to foot. Still, he had mentioned the basket. It hung heavy on her arm and she was suddenly certain he knew the diamond necklace was inside.

Sarah glanced toward the doorway, wondering if

she should make a run for it. She was five-six and had run the hurdles in high school, but Michael had a good eight inches on her and a powerful, athletic body. She should know since she'd stared at it often enough when he'd walked through the bank to his private elevator. All the women had stared. Though he'd seemed as oblivious of the drooling female admiration as he had of her.

Until now. Michael stood with his legs wide apart, a long tail hanging between them. The wolf costume hugged his body, looking as if it had been custom-made. It probably had. No, running wasn't a good idea. He'd probably tackle her before she even made it to the door.

He bared straight, white teeth in a wolfish smile. "These woods are dangerous for such a tasty little morsel like yourself. Did you get lost on your way to grandmother's house, my dear?"

Sarah blinked, suddenly realizing he hadn't recognized her after all. He was simply playing the part of the Big, Bad Wolf to her Little Red Riding Hood. She'd better relax and play along, too, if she didn't want to arouse his suspicion.

"I decided to take the scenic tour," she replied, meeting his intense gaze, "although the woods are certainly getting crowded these days."

He looked around the ballroom. "Very true. But at

the moment I don't find any of these people nearly as enticing as you."

The husky tenor of his voice made her palms grow damp in her gloves. Was the man actually flirting with her? Despite her plan to break into a safe tonight, she'd never been attracted to danger. But something about the heavy shadow of whiskers on his square jaw and the way his gray eyes glittered behind the slits of the black silk mask intrigued her.

"I'll bet you say that to all the girls who get lost in your woods."

He took a step closer to her. "The woods can be a dangerous place."

"I don't scare easily."

"But I'm a very hungry wolf." He took another step toward her. "I could feast my eyes on you all night."

She heard it again. The husky undertone that told her his interest was more than casual. Sarah hadn't been on the receiving end of this kind of undivided male attention for a very long time. She found the experience as intoxicating as the champagne bubbling from the fountain in the middle of the ballroom.

But she also knew about Michael's notorious reputation with women. "Be careful, Mr. Wolff. I might give you heartburn."

"Impossible," he countered with a smile that made her stomach drop. "I don't have a heart."

She'd heard that, too, but the admission didn't seem to bother him. And no doubt the man had broken plenty of hearts himself. Was he as ruthless in love as he was in business? His skills as the CEO of Wolff Enterprises had recently been featured in both the *Wall Street Journal* and *Fortune* magazine. Both articles had made the rounds among her fellow bank employees shortly after he'd acquired the parent company of Consolidated Bank.

"You, on the other hand," he said, leaning closer to her, "probably have too big a heart. Don't you ever just want to let old granny take care of herself so you can have time to play?"

His words hit the mark closer than she wanted to admit. Her family meant everything to her. That's why she was here, risking her future, instead of out with her friends celebrating New Year's Eve. She'd already made some resolutions for the upcoming year. *Be spontaneous. Take more risks. Date.*

That last one was difficult to do while working two jobs. But her reaction to Michael's simple flirtation tonight was proof that she'd been out of the dating circuit too long.

Her skin actually tingled when his appreciative gaze once again drifted below her neck. She found herself wondering how his whiskers would feel against her cheek. How his broad hand would feel on her body.

It had been *much* too long. She needed to put some distance between them before she made a complete fool of herself. "Granny is depending on me." She motioned toward the buffet table. "I'll just fill up my basket with some goodies, then be on my way."

Sarah wanted to kick herself as soon as the words were out of her mouth. *Why had she mentioned the basket?* She saw his gaze move toward her arm where the wicker basket hung, its valuable contents hidden beneath the lid. All he had to do was open it to see the vintage blue velvet jewelry case inside. What if he recognized it?

Then all hell would break loose.

Michael grabbed two glasses of champagne from a passing waiter. He handed one of them to her. "Have a drink with me first. To celebrate the New Year."

Michael Wolff had already clouded her thinking. The last thing she needed was alcohol. "Thank you," she replied, setting it back on the tray. "I don't drink."

"Such a good girl," he murmured, a feral glimmer in his gray eyes. Then he lifted the champagne flute to his lips.

She started to contradict him, then realized he was right. She'd been good forever. When you grew up in a household with a sick grandmother and a felonious grandfather, you learned not to make trouble for your parents. So she'd been a straight-A student in school, then paid her own way through college with a series of scholarships, grants and student loans.

When her father's business had transferred him and her mother to California last year, she'd moved from an apartment back into the family home to take care of her grandfather—a task made all the more difficult when he decided to come out of retirement and start stealing again. Small wonder she had no time for a social life.

Sarah watched Michael's firm mouth curl around the rim of the crystal flute as he tipped back his head. The muscles in his throat flexed as he swallowed, then he lowered the flute, and his feral gray eyes met hers once more. "We had the champagne flown in from France. You don't know what you're missing."

How she wanted to give into temptation. Even the way he drank champagne was sexy. But she couldn't afford to lose her head, not over champagne and not over Michael.

"I think I do," she replied, turning away from him. "Goodbye, Mr. Wolff."

He grasped her elbow, the gentle pressure of his fingers sending a flush of heat through her body. "Dance with me, Red."

When she hesitated, he moved closer and whispered, "I see Oscar Henley heading my way and if you don't dance with me I will have to listen to his excruciatingly long audit story again. He's such an awful storyteller, I actually root for the IRS each time I hear it."

She smiled. "He does seem to like the sound of his own voice."

Michael arched a brow. "So you know Oscar?"

Sarah mentally cringed. Oscar was on the board of directors at Consolidated Bank. So much for trying to remain anonymous. Maybe she could bluff her way out of it. "Doesn't everyone?"

He laughed. "Yes. Whether they want to or not." Then he pulled her into his arms. "So you have to rescue me."

"Little Red Riding Hood rescuing the wolf," she mused, her common sense telling her this was madness, her curiosity making her unable to walk away. "Now that's a definite twist to the story."

The music was slow and seductive. He tried to pull her close, but the picnic basket got in the way. Michael gently slipped it off her arm before she could react and a spasm of panic enveloped her. But he simply set the basket on the edge of the bandstand, then turned back to dance with her.

Was she crazy? She never should have let him take the basket away from her. Never should have accepted his invitation to dance. She'd planned to blend into the gold brocade wallpaper this evening, slipping upstairs when the clock struck midnight to complete her mission.

Now she was in his arms, her cheek pressed against his broad, furry shoulder. She closed her eyes as they swayed to the music, thinking he smelled quite nice for a wolf. Spicy and masculine.

Sarah certainly hadn't planned to capture the attention of big, bad Michael Wolff. But as the evocative music swelled around her, she slowly began to relax. What could one dance hurt? For the past two years, she'd found herself watching Michael Wolff every time he'd walked into Consolidated Bank. Even fantasized about him a little. Okay, a lot. So why not take advantage of the opportunity to fulfill one of those fantasies?

Best of all, she could do it anonymously. Michael would never know the identity of Little Red Riding Hood because she planned to be long gone before the unveiling at midnight.

He tightened his arms around her and his warm breath circled her ear, sending delicious shivers throughout her body. "This is nice."

"You sound surprised."

His deep chuckle reverberated in his chest. "I've never been a big fan of masquerade parties. I don't like playing games, especially when it's so easy to guess who's behind the mask." He pulled away slightly to meet her gaze. "Except for you, Red. I have to admit I'm stumped."

She intended for him to stay that way. If Michael knew her real identity, she'd be booted out the door. The Wolffs and the Hewitts were sworn enemies, at least according to her grandfather. Maybe that's the reason Michael Wolff had always held such a fascination for her.

Besides, she and Michael lived in completely different worlds. He was crème brûlée while she was cream of wheat. It made the fact that they were dancing together all the more unbelievable.

"Why not just enjoy the fantasy?" she said at last. "No names. No questions. No promises. Just two strangers dancing in the night."

Heat flashed in his eyes. "In my fantasy, we do more than dance."

She *never* should have come here tonight. "Really?"

He lifted one hand and slowly slid the tip of his finger over the curve of her cheek, then across her lower lip. "Like I said before, it's dangerous in these woods."

His sensuous touch made her lips tingle. "I'm not afraid."

"Liar," he whispered huskily, then cupped her cheek in his broad hand. "But I'll keep you safe. Just come back with me to my lair."

She took a deep breath, her heart pounding even harder now, but not with fear. "My, what a big ego you have."

He smiled. "That's not all."

She laughed in spite of herself. "Thank you for the invitation, but I think it will be much safer here in the woods."

"That's where you're wrong, Red."

Then he kissed her.

2

SWEET.

That was the first word that came into Michael's mind when he kissed her, his mouth tasting those lush pink lips that had tempted him from the first moment he'd set eyes on her tonight.

Innocent.

He'd caught her startled gasp in his mouth when his lips had molded to hers. He glimpsed the uncertainty in her beautiful green eyes. The desire, too. It fueled his own, his body on fire now as he pulled her even closer to him.

Perfect.

Maybe it was the imported champagne, or the incredible stress of the past few weeks. Maybe he'd simply gone too long without a woman in his arms, in his bed. Whatever the reason, Michael simply couldn't remember a kiss so perfect before. So right.

She clung to his shoulders as he deepened the kiss, her hands fisting in the fur of his costume. After a moment, her lips softened, parted. Giving him entry to her mouth. So sweet. So innocent. So perfect.

The woman made him insatiable. He wanted more, so much more. But the sound of glasses clinking and the rumble of voices around them finally sifted through his lust-fogged brain, telling him this wasn't the time or the place to pursue his fantasy.

Michael lifted his head and tried to breathe normally. The wolf costume, which had been unbearably itchy all night, now was even more so, thanks to the heat generated by that kiss.

His Red Riding Hood blinked up at him, her green eyes wide and her lips now as red as her cape. His gaze quickly scanned the room, aware of a few knowing smiles and furtive whispers. Michael was used to gossips, though he usually tried to avoid giving them firsthand grist for the mill.

What the hell had come over him?

Red wasn't even his type. He liked his women sultry and sophisticated, tall and tempestuous. She barely reached his shoulder. He wouldn't have even approached her tonight if he hadn't seen her standing alone in the middle of the ballroom, looking as lost as he often felt.

Yet, he wanted her. Wanted her so damn much that now he took another step back just to keep from reaching for her again.

She cleared her throat, a pretty pink blush sweeping over her cheeks. "The music is over."

The music might be over, but not the fantasy. Now

he wanted to do more than dance with her, more than kiss her. But not in front of a hundred guests. He wanted Red all to himself.

Someone called out his name and Michael turned around to see Oscar Henley hailing him again. He clenched his jaw, knowing he couldn't escape this time.

She noticed Oscar, too, and smiled up at Michael. "Duty calls."

Duty. Michael had lived it every day of his life. As the only heir to the Wolff dynasty, it was his duty to make certain the family business thrived, to direct and expand Wolff Enterprises, to protect the family fortune.

A fortune that could be in jeopardy, thanks to his grandfather's lovely young wife. Michael should be focused on that tonight instead of losing his head over a mysterious lady in red.

But he found himself reluctant to let go of her so soon. *No names. No questions. No promises.* Those were her terms and they had intrigued him before that incredible kiss. But now...now he wanted to know her name. Wanted to know everything about her.

And he realized she must be aware of his identity. It was tradition for the host of the Wolff Ball to dress as a wolf. Usually that was his grandfather's role. But Seamus was in the hospital tonight, recovering from a broken hip.

Thanks to his lovely young wife.

Tension coiled inside of him, but Michael couldn't think about the Wolff family problems right now. He didn't *want* to think about them. Not with Red standing so close, her subtle vanilla scent driving him wild. It reminded him of her kiss. So sweet and innocent. Michael closed his eyes, his duty battling with his desire. He wanted nothing more than to whisk her far away from here, to leave behind all the problems and the decisions and the responsibilities that came with the Wolff name.

Oscar called out to him again and Michael opened his eyes to see the stocky man making his way across the ballroom floor. He swallowed a sigh. "I suppose I have to play the good host for a while."

She nodded. "Thank you for the dance."

That sounded too much like goodbye. He grasped both her hands in his own, his thumbs smoothing over the crinkled red silk of her gloves. "Meet me at midnight. Right here. In front of the bandstand."

He wanted to be there when she removed her mask. He wanted to see her face.

She licked her lips, her hesitation telling him that she was going to refuse. He couldn't give her that chance.

"No names," he assured her, wondering at her skittishness. "No questions."

"No promises," she whispered.

"Midnight," he repeated, gently squeezing her hands. Then he turned and walked away.

Midnight couldn't come soon enough for him.

TEN MINUTES TILL MIDNIGHT.

Sarah was lost. She'd planned this nocturnal excursion into the Wolff mansion down to the last detail, memorizing every room, every staircase, every winding hallway. There was only one thing she hadn't planned on—Michael Wolff.

Sensing his gaze on her across the ballroom, Sarah had changed her plan at the last minute, choosing a route via the ladies' room instead of taking the main staircase to the third floor.

From there she found a back staircase that led to the second floor. She knew from the blueprints that here she would find the library, offices and a long gallery full of priceless art. She had to find the staircase leading to the third floor, where the private rooms were located.

Only that staircase was closed for renovation. Sarah stood in the dark hallway, trying not to panic. If only that kiss hadn't left her so confused and disoriented. So...unsatisfied. She raised her fingers to her lips, still slightly swollen.

Meet me at midnight.

His words echoed in her ears and she leaned against the wall a moment to collect herself. What if she hadn't been here under false pretenses, but was actually an invited guest? What if they truly were two strangers dancing in the night? What if she met him at midnight...?

Sarah shook those thoughts from her head. She couldn't afford to indulge in fantasies, no matter how tempting. She needed to save her grandfather. Grasping the picnic basket more tightly, she surveyed her surroundings, then took a left down the hallway.

Her planned route was useless now and the longer it took to find the right floor, much less the right room, the more nervous she became. When she thought she'd finally found it, she ended up standing in a huge linen closet.

"Okay, take a breath," she muttered to herself, inhaling the starchy scent of neatly folded sheets and pillowcases. Closing her eyes, she pictured the floor plans once more in her mind. If she was in the second floor linen closet, then she needed to take a right at the next hallway, then a left. That should lead her to the servants' staircase at the back of the mansion.

As she hurried down the hallway, she found herself wondering what Michael would do when she stood him up at the bandstand. Would he be angry? Disappointed? If so, she knew it wouldn't take him long to find another woman to take her place.

But Sarah didn't want to think about that, not

when she could still taste his champagne kiss on her lips and still remember the gentle way he'd touched her. That's what surprised her the most—his gentleness. So at odds with his ruthless reputation.

Sarah turned a corner and was relieved to see the servants' staircase directly in front of her. Quickly mounting the steps, she could only hope she didn't run into a servant along the way.

Once on the third floor, she took a moment to get her bearings. It was dark, the long hallway lit by a lone sconce at the far end. She was close enough to the light switch to reach out and flip it on, but she didn't dare risk calling attention to her presence up here.

Especially with Michael Wolff on the prowl.

FIVE MINUTES TILL MIDNIGHT.

Michael stood off by himself in the crowded ballroom and sipped his fifth glass of champagne. He kept checking the time, watching the seconds drag by.

As usual, many of the guests had approached him for a financial donation. Michael's growing reputation as a philanthropist made him the target for every get-rich scheme out there. Most people believed he gave his money away for tax purposes—a fallacy he didn't bother to correct. Michael was no saint, he just didn't need any more money.

So he gave it to foster-care programs and pediatric research hospitals. Made anonymous donations to local shelters and urban-redevelopment programs. Unfortunately, the size of those gifts had been leaked to the media, whose tenacious digging revealed him as the benefactor.

Now everyone in Denver knew Michael liked to give his money away. Both friends and strangers approached him for donations—to either their favorite charity or, more often, their latest business investment.

Tonight, those solicitations for cash also came with questions about the woman he'd kissed on the dance floor—questions he deftly avoided, not only to protect his privacy, but simply because he didn't know the answers.

To his surprise, Michael discovered that he wasn't the only one stumped by Little Red Riding Hood's true identity. Many of the other guests, especially the single women, kept trying to place her. But, so far, none had been successful, which just made her more intriguing in his eyes. More mysterious.

Four minutes till midnight.

Even Blair had asked him about her. His grandfather's wife usually paid little attention to his social life, probably because she disliked him as much as he disliked her. No, that wasn't true. Michael didn't dislike her. He just didn't trust her. With good reason.

His gaze moved slowly over the ballroom until he spotted Mrs. Seamus Wolff, resplendent in her elaborate Cleopatra costume. A former hand model, she was tall and slender, with long, sleek black hair that fit perfectly with her exotic costume.

He didn't have any actual proof that she'd arranged that accident on the stairs. Yet. But it wasn't the first accident to befall his grandfather in the six weeks since he'd changed his will. Seamus had also careened into a ditch with his vintage Packard, thanks to a faulty brake line. Either accident could have been fatal—which would have made Blair Wolff a very rich woman.

Only thirty-four, Blair Ballingham Wolff had been married to his seventy-year-old grandfather for almost three years. She was wife number six. Seamus jokingly described himself as a serial husband, divorcing his wives when they got too old for him.

But the truth was that Seamus's first five wives had taken the easy escape route after only a few months of matrimony, collecting the one-hundred-thousand dollars promised them in the premarital agreement. An unusual agreement in that they only received the money if the marriage lasted less than one year. If it lasted more than a year, they received nothing. So far, all of them had preferred taking the cash to living with an extremely cranky, albeit very rich, old man.

All of them except Blair. Her loyalty had impressed Seamus so much that he'd actually changed his will recently, leaving her a sizable portion of the Wolff estate, certainly much more than a measly hundred grand. But was Blair truly loyal to Seamus or just greedier—and deadlier—than his other wives? That's what Michael intended to find out— before it was too late.

Three minutes till midnight.

He drained his glass, aware once again that the Wolff fortune proved both a blessing and a curse. He had more money than he could ever spend. Unlimited opportunities. Yet, just like his grandfather, he could never afford the one thing that every person on the planet sought. Love. Because he'd never know for certain if a woman truly loved him or just his well-padded wallet.

That didn't mean he'd given up on women entirely. He definitely enjoyed female companionship, especially in his bed. As long as they understood that sex didn't equal love or commitment. He always made that perfectly clear before embarking on any new relationship, though most women still believed they could trap a Wolff. So far, he'd proven them all wrong.

Two minutes till midnight.

His wolf costume prickled against the bare skin of his back. He resisted the urge to squirm against the wall, desperate for relief from the agonizing itch that had been aggravated by the heat-inducing dance with Red. He'd stared into her mossy green eyes—eyes as lush and mysterious as a virgin forest. And he'd been the one in danger of getting lost there.

He longed for another slow dance with Red. A private slow dance.

Michael let his gaze wander around the ballroom, but he didn't see her scarlet cape anywhere. What kind of body did that cape hide? What color hair under that hood? What secrets behind her smile?

One minute till midnight.

Michael pushed himself off the wall and headed toward the bandstand, slipping unobtrusively through the raucous crowd of guests. He wanted to see her face during the unveiling. To formally meet the woman who had turned down the invitation to his lair. He'd been half joking at the time, but her refusal had enthralled him. Maybe she truly didn't recognize him. Or she simply wasn't impressed by his wealth. Maybe money didn't matter to her.

Michael wished he could still believe in fairy tales.

At last the clock struck midnight. He turned in a slow circle, his heart beating double time. Colorful balloons and confetti floated down from the ceiling to celebrate the dawn of the New Year. Couples embraced around him. Champagne corks popped. He removed his mask, but he couldn't see his Red anywhere.

Maybe she'd gotten lost in his woods after all.

MIDNIGHT.

The first deep gong reverberated through the mansion. Sarah froze, her hand on the doorknob of the room containing the safe. Michael would be in front of the bandstand now, watching for her. Waiting. But how long would he wait?

The second gong sounded a heartbeat later and Sarah knew she didn't have time to waste. She bent down to jimmy the lock, a trick taught to her by her grandfather. On the third gong, she slipped inside the room, quietly closing the door behind her. She locked it, then turned around, her pulse racing.

Her leather boots sunk into the deep, plush carpet as the fourth gong rang out. The air smelled faintly of sandalwood, but the room itself was pitch-black, without even a hint of moonlight.

The thick darkness unnerved her as the sound of the fifth gong echoed through the mansion. She fumbled inside the picnic basket for the miniature flashlight she'd purchased just this afternoon. At last she found it and switched it on.

The sixth gong drowned out her groan when nothing happened. She rapidly flipped the flashlight switch back and forth, hoping for a miracle. But no such luck. Either the new flashlight or the new batteries she'd purchased for it were defective. She wanted to kick herself for not testing it before now.

At the seventh gong, she skimmed one hand blindly along the wall for a light switch, then turned it on for the length of the eighth, ninth and tenth gongs, just long enough for her gaze to sweep along the wall, taking note of the small marble table and the chaise lounge shaped like a chariot underneath the window. In the middle of the room stood a gold tent. Odd. But Sarah didn't have time to satisfy her curiosity by taking a closer look.

At the eleventh gong, she flipped off the wall switch, fearing someone passing by might see the light filtering under the door and become suspicious. She was probably more paranoid than necessary, but Sarah simply couldn't stand the thought of discovery.

The twelfth gong rang out as she considered the consequences of what she was about to do. If caught, she'd not only lose her job, but the publicity would be humiliating. She'd lose the respect of her friends. Her co-workers. Michael.

Especially Michael.

It was silly, perhaps, since they'd never even been formally introduced. All they'd shared tonight was a dance and a kiss. A wonderful kiss.

Still, she didn't want to imagine the expression on his face if he discovered his Little Red Riding Hood had broken into the family safe. Her best bet was to get moving so she'd be gone before the party broke up.

Gripping the picnic basket more tightly, she began to slowly walk along the wall, running the fingers of her free hand along the crevices. According to her grandfather, the safe was located somewhere between the window and the door, with a telltale fissure in the seam of the panel walls to indicate the hidden steel compartment underneath—a fissure that a person could only discern by touch.

Her grandfather had shared every detail of his diamond necklace heist, with a little prodding from Sarah. She'd felt a little guilty about it, especially since he was so darn proud of his success. So thrilled to give her what he truly believed to be her rightful legacy.

But Sarah couldn't keep the necklace. Her conscience wouldn't allow it and her grandfather's growing bitterness over the years simply blinded him to that fact. He was so certain that the necklace could change her future. That it could have changed the past. That it could have saved her grandmother.

Sarah knew she could never convince him otherwise. So she had given up trying. And if her grandfather ever asked her about the diamond necklace, she'd simply tell him she'd put it in safekeeping. That would be the truth. The Wolff safe was the only place secure enough to keep Bertram Hewitt out of prison.

Her wandering thoughts made her forget about the small marble table in her path. She bumped her knee against it, causing the lamp on top of it to teeter precariously. She caught it just in time to prevent it from crashing to the floor.

She could just picture shattered glass on the carpet, a sure indication that someone had been in here. Sarah would prefer the Wolffs never suspected an intruder had entered this room. She didn't want anything possibly leading the police to either her or her grandfather. Bertram had assured her that he hadn't left any fingerprints behind a week ago, but with the sophistication of DNA testing, she couldn't be certain he hadn't left some identifying physical evidence in this room.

Carefully setting the lamp upright again, Sarah heaved an impatient sigh. The room was too big and she simply didn't want to take the chance of bumping into something else. Despite the risks, she had to turn on the lamp to get her bearings.

Running her fingers along the lead crystal base, she found the switch and turned it on. Soft light spilled across the room and she saw now what she hadn't the time to see before. It was a bedroom. The tent was actually a round canopy bed with heavy gold drapes concealing everything but the ornate sandalwood headboard.

The room resembled a desert oasis, with the thick carpet the color of sand and a trickling limestone fountain in one corner. Potted palm trees lined the far wall and the ceiling was painted a serene sky blue. The walls themselves were made of bleached pine paneling, with hieroglyphics painted on various portions. It truly was the oddest bedroom she'd ever seen.

Turning back to the wall once more, she moved her hand swiftly along the paneling until her fingers finally detected a grainy pattern in the crevice of the wood different from the rest.

Sarah pressed hard on the crease and the secret wall panel popped open, revealing the safe underneath. She set the picnic basket on the floor, then took a deep breath, preparing to disconnect the alarm wire. This was the trickiest part of the whole process. If she tripped the alarm...

"Don't go there," Sarah chastised herself. Just as in any other profession, to be successful, a safecracker had to think positively.

A moment later, she breathed a sigh of relief. The alarm wire was disconnected. All she had to do now was open the safe, place the diamond necklace back inside, then leave by the back entrance of the mansion. No doubt the party would still be in full swing, so no one would be the wiser.

Was Michael still waiting for her? Or had he already moved onto someone else?

Sarah turned the dial, grateful her grandfather had revealed the combination when he'd bragged about his heist. He'd taught her how to crack a safe, a skill he'd learned from some of his more unsavory customers at the pawnshop. But that would take time that she simply didn't have.

"Fifty-four," she murmured under her breath, her voice sounding odd to her ears.

She reversed the direction of the dial. "Thirteen."

So far, so good. But at the sound of heavy footsteps out in the hallway, she hesitated, her entire body tensing. They stopped right outside the door.

She silently closed the secret wall panel, her heart beating so fast she thought she might pass out. But the sound of someone jiggling the brass doorknob shocked her enough to remain conscious. She looked desperately around the room, wondering where she could possibly hide. The sound of keys jingling told her she didn't have much time to decide.

Someone was coming in.

3

MICHAEL JAMMED the key into the lock, the incessant itching almost driving him to the point of madness. He slammed the door open, then tore off the top half of the costume before he even turned on the light. Buttons popped and hit the wall, but he didn't care. He flung the furry shirt halfway across his bedroom.

Frustration roiled inside of him. He'd looked everywhere for her—combed every inch of the ballroom, then broadened his search to include the entire first floor. He'd even interrogated the doorman. But it was no use.

She was gone.

It was these stupid costumes. Never again. He didn't care if it was tradition for the host of the Wolff Ball to dress as a wolf. If Seamus didn't want the role next New Year's Eve, they could damn well forego the costumes and dress in tuxedos like normal people. He'd always thought the masquerade part of the ball was ridiculous anyway.

He never should have let her go. Now he had no way of identifying his Little Red Riding Hood. His only option was to go over the guest list tomorrow and try to establish her identity by process of elimination.

But that wouldn't change the fact that she'd stood him up for their midnight rendezvous. Michael wasn't used to chasing women. They usually came to him.

Until tonight.

Maybe she wasn't even on the guest list. Had she come with someone? Another man? That possibility hadn't occurred to him until now. It didn't quite fit, though, since no man had objected when Michael had kissed her on the dance floor. If he'd seen his woman mauled by a wolf, he sure as hell would have made his presence known.

He reached out to turn on the light, then realized he could already see. The lamp was on. Odd, since he never used it. One of the maids must have left it on.

Michael sat down on the chaise lounge and stripped off his boots, socks and furry pants, tossing them all into a heap on the floor. Relief at last. Tomorrow the entire costume would go straight into the trash.

He stood up and walked over to the dresser, reaching for the centuries-old bronze spear hanging on the wall above it. Blair had purchased the spear in her latest redecorating binge. She was into Egyptian decor this month and his bedroom had suffered the consequences.

In his opinion, she'd gone overboard with the depraved sheik look. Another not-so-subtle message that she didn't approve of him. Or perhaps an attempt to finally drive him out of the house. Blair had mentioned more than once that a twenty-nine-year-old man should not be living with his grandfather.

Neither should a thirty-four-year-old woman, but he mostly kept that opinion to himself. He also ignored Blair's hints that he move into the city. Someone had to stay and watch over his grandfather.

Seamus Wolff had raised Michael since he was almost thirteen years old, helping him to care about life again after his father's private jet crashed during an impulsive weekend ski trip to Vail. Seamus was the only family Michael had left in the world—the only family that counted, anyway. And he damn well intended to do whatever it took to protect the old man.

Michael raked the end of the bronze spear across his back, moaning aloud with pleasure as he satisfied the itch that had plagued him all evening. The spear had brought close to two thousand dollars at a Sotheby's auction—one hell of an expensive back scratcher.

Music floated up from the ballroom two floors below and he knew he should return to the party until the last guest walked out the door. But he just couldn't stand the thought of putting that suffocating wolf costume back on. Or making small talk. Or parrying the flirtations of the inebriated women downstairs.

There was only one woman he wanted.

Smoothing one hand over his bare chest, he wished like hell he'd never stopped kissing her. But Michael didn't believe in regrets. Time to forget about her and move on. He'd done it before.

He laid the spear on top of his dresser, then padded over to the window to open the drapes. Moonlight cast an ethereal glow over the room. He turned to switch off the lamp and, for the first time, he caught a vanilla scent in the air that reminded him of Little Red Riding Hood. Her perfume must have clung to his costume.

Picking up the furry shirt, he held it to his nose and inhaled deeply. But all it did was make him sneeze. "Give it up, Wolff," he muttered, dropping the shirt on the floor once more.

He padded barefoot to the ridiculous harem tent bed, already dreading the long day that lay ahead tomorrow. His grandfather would be coming home from the hospital, and that would make him vulnerable to another "accident." Michael would have to be more vigilant than ever.

As he pulled back the heavy gold canopy drape,

the alluring vanilla scent assailed him again, only much stronger now. He blinked when he saw the reason for it sitting on his bed.

Red had ventured into his lair after all.

THIS WAS NOT GOOD.

Sarah should have realized her mission to return the diamond necklace was doomed when that stupid flashlight didn't work.

No, even before that, when she'd found the back stairway under construction. She should have turned around at that moment and walked right out the door. Now she had to find some way to extricate herself from this sensitive situation before Michael got the wrong idea.

Judging by his expression, it was already too late. "My, what big eyes you have," he said, standing beside the bed in nothing but a pair of black boxer shorts. The sight of his powerful body sent her already frazzled nerves into complete disarray.

Sarah could hardly think straight, much less speak. At last she recovered enough to form a sentence. "I think that's my line."

His brawny shoulders and rippling muscles belied the fact that this man worked behind a desk. The dark, silky hair matting his chest tantalized her, but her hands fisted into the sheets as he loomed closer.

She knew he'd be as dangerous to touch as a real wolf.

It was a danger that strangely appealed to her.

Sarah sucked in a deep breath. "I shouldn't be here."

"But I'm so glad you are." He reached out one broad hand and lightly traced the length of the red glove encasing her left arm.

His touch was hypnotic. Her gaze followed his hand as it trailed up her forearm, then down again. She should make some kind of excuse, jump out of this bed and run right out the door.

Only the diamond necklace was still in her picnic basket, and that basket sat directly beneath the safe. If she left it behind, could Michael find a way to trace it to her? She needed time to think. A new plan.

But thought became impossible when Michael leaned even closer, the canopy drape falling closed behind him so that they were now enclosed in silky darkness. Only the barest hint of light glowed behind the golden drapes.

Michael's face was hidden in the shadows, which just made everything seem more unreal. More dreamlike.

Until he kissed her. The taste of him was very real. Dizzying. Delicious. His warm, firm mouth skimmed her lips in a way that actually made her lean into him for more.

A low growl rumbled in his throat as he deepened the kiss and she had to grab his broad shoulders to keep from falling back on the bed. Her fingers encountered warm skin and hard muscle that flexed beneath her touch.

Michael moved beside her on the bed, never breaking the kiss, as his fingers slid down the length of her throat to the bow tied at the collar of her cloak. He worked it with his fingers until it loosened, the fabric gaping to reveal the red silk blouse she wore underneath.

He broke the kiss and used both hands to reverently lower the hood, revealing her hair tied back in a ponytail. He released it, so that her wayward dark curls hung about her face. Winding one loosely around his index finger, he brushed it against the rough whiskers on his jaw.

"Soft." His voice was husky, his eyes intense.

Desire pooled low in her belly as Michael slid her cloak off her shoulders, his hungry gaze roaming over her body.

Sarah reached out one hand, but instead of pushing him away, she placed her palm flat against his chest. The silky hair there trickled between her fingers. Her touch made his chest muscles contract and she could feel the fast gallop of his heart beneath her hand.

Almost as fast as her own. "My, what big muscles

you have," she whispered, knowing instinctively how risky it was to tease a wolf. But Sarah couldn't seem to stop herself. She didn't *want* to stop.

"All the better to hold you with, my dear." Then Michael kissed her again, even more hungrily this time. He enveloped her shoulders with his grip, the warmth of his big hands seeping through the thin silk of her blouse.

He pulled her closer, until her body was flush against his own. Silk against skin. Soft against hard. The intimate contact made her long for more. Made her forget everything but this man. This moment.

As his mouth devoured her, his fingers stalked the buttons of her blouse. The zipper on her skirt. Until she wore nothing but her lacy red bra and panties, lingerie bought on a whim yesterday to implement her New Year's resolution to take more risks. No more boring beige underwear.

No more boring beige life.

"My, what big hands you have," she gasped as his touches became more intimate.

She could sense rather than see his predatory smile.

"All the better to ravish you with, my dear."

Then he did just that, but with a fierce tenderness that both touched and aroused her. Michael's big hands peeled away her bra with such sensual skill that Sarah thought she must be dreaming.

Then those incredible hands moved lower.

A midnight madness now consumed her and she simply couldn't think at all anymore. Only feel. The hard length of his body pressed against her. The skilled pressure of his hands. The urgent heat of his kisses.

Soon they were both naked. Both voracious. Both hunting for the pleasure they knew they'd only find in each other.

Michael tasted every inch of her. His tongue stroking her breasts. Her belly. The inside of her thighs. His ravenous exploration of her body driving her wild. A wildness he seemed to share when she did the same to him.

"Oh, Red," he moaned, his breath coming in short pants as her hair swept over his belly. Strangled groans of desire emanated from deep in his chest.

At last, Michael pulled her up to kiss him. Frantically. Reverently. Her naked body now lay atop his own and she wasn't surprised to find they fit perfectly together.

Then he rolled her under him, reaching into a drawer and retrieving a condom in the same movement. He tore it open with his teeth, then inhaled a choked breath as she slowly rolled it on him.

When he reached up to remove her mask, she shook her head, determined to remain anonymous, to perpetuate the fantasy. They were two strangers in the night. *No names. No questions. No promises.*

Only Michael did make promises. With his hands. His mouth. His body. At last he sank into her, moving with deliberate slowness to draw out the exquisiteness of the moment. She'd never made love like this before. Never with so much savage hunger. So much need. So much passion. Animal passion that now consumed her, bringing out her most primal instincts. Her hands raked across his back as he brought her to the brink of ecstasy.

"Michael," she cried, wanting more of him. All of him.

"Red," he breathed, sweeping his lips across her mouth and shifting his body in a way that heightened the incredible sensations twisting through her.

It was enough to send her over the edge.

She took him with her, his body tensing in her arms, then shuddering with one final thrust. He buried his face in the crook of her neck, his breathing as harsh and uneven as her own. When at last he collected himself, he turned onto his side, pulling her with him.

"I won't let you go," he whispered, even as his eyelids drooped. His arm tightened around her, pulling her even closer.

Sarah relaxed against him, all her nerve endings still thrumming. The warmth of his large body enveloped her like a cocoon. She closed her eyes for a moment, still caught up in the fantasy, one she knew had to end very soon. But not yet.

Not quite yet.

SARAH AWOKE SLOWLY the next morning, the rays of the morning sun streaming through the open drapes. She winced at the brightness, yawned lazily, then suddenly she realized that she was naked beneath the silk sheets.

Naked in Michael Wolff's arms.

Panic hit her like a jolt of caffeine. She'd fallen asleep last night. She hadn't returned the necklace to the safe. She was in *big* trouble.

Her body tensed as she listened to the sound of Michael's deep, even breathing. At least he was still asleep. She might still have a chance to make her escape before he awoke.

Carefully extricating herself from his arms, she slipped soundlessly out of the big round bed. How could she have fallen asleep last night? She remembered lying in his embrace, waiting for him to drift off. The warmth of his naked body pressed against her. The sated afterglow of her own. The dreamy visions of more nights together.

A dream that could never come true.

Instead, she'd created her own nightmare. She'd proved beyond all doubt that she wasn't cut out for a life of crime—as if sleeping with her family's arch-enemy hadn't already done that.

But Sarah couldn't let herself think about that now. She had to get dressed, get the necklace back in the safe, then get the hell out of there.

She frantically searched for the clothes he'd stripped off of her the night before. All she could find were her panties, bra, boots and the cloak. Her gloves, blouse and skirt had to still be in the bed with him.

Not willing to take the risk of waking him, she hastily pulled on her bra and panties, then tied the wrinkled red cloak around her neck. She placed her boots in the picnic basket, deciding not to put them on until she was out of the house. Her exit needed to be as silent as possible.

Her basket still sat directly beneath the safe. Thankfully, Michael hadn't noticed it there last night or he might have gotten suspicious. He might have questioned her in his bed instead of making love to her there.

Memories of the night before washed over her, warming her cheeks. In the light of day, making love to Michael Wolff seemed like a huge mistake. But she'd worry about that later. *After* she was out of his house.

Padding silently to the safe, she slowly opened the panel. The slight squeal made her wince. Casting a glance over her shoulder, she didn't see any movement from the bed, though the canopy drapes obscured her vision of Michael. She hoped he was a deep sleeper.

Fifty-four. Telling herself not to rush it, Sarah turned the dial on the safe, her fingers sensing the slight give in the tension of the dial when she reached the first number of the combination.

Thirteen. She reversed the direction of the dial, hearing her own rapid heartbeat in her ears.

Sixty-one. She heard the satisfying click as she reached the last number. Almost there.

Sarah slowly swung open the heavy steel door of the safe, thankful it didn't squeak. Then she bent down and reached inside her basket for the worn velvet jewelry case, a case she hoped to never lay eyes on again.

Sarah carefully set the velvet case deep inside the safe, releasing a deep breath she didn't know she'd been holding.

Then Michael's cold, harsh voice turned her blood to ice. "What the hell do you think you're doing?"

4

MICHAEL COULDN'T BELIEVE his eyes. He blinked, certain he must be dreaming—or in the midst of some horrific nightmare. Red was standing there with her hand inside his safe.

He catapulted out of the bed, flinging the heavy canopy drapes back behind him. He watched her beautiful green eyes drop down his body and realized too late that he was still naked.

But he was too furious to care.

"You still haven't answered my question," he said, barely able to keep his voice below a roar.

She still wore the red mask, along with the red cloak, though the hood was down. Her silky dark hair spilled wildly over her shoulders.

He remembered the sensation of that hair on his skin last night when she'd explored his body with her mouth. *Sweet torture.*

Michael hastily turned around and grabbed his bulky terry cloth robe off the hook near the bed, pulling it on before she could see the effect the sensual memory had on him.

When he faced her again, her green eyes met his through the mask and he saw her swallow.

"I...I..."

Michael waited, hoping she'd come up with a rational explanation. Anything but the obvious—that she'd slept with him for his money, just like all the rest. Unlike the others, Red hadn't been patient enough to see if she could seduce him into falling in love with her.

Obviously, she wanted the payout a lot sooner.

"You're good," he bit out, realizing last night had been a fantasy in more ways than one. "Very good. You've got that little Miss Innocent act down pat. I never would have guessed you were a common thief."

"I'm not!" She took a deep breath. "I can explain."

"Don't bother." He folded his arms across his chest, letting his anger override his bitter disappointment. "You're right, of course. A common thief doesn't normally seduce her victims before committing the crime. That takes a very callous and calculating thief."

"*You* seduced *me*," she retorted, her eyes flashing. "I certainly never intended for anything like that to happen between us."

He arched a brow. "Then why were you waiting for me in my bed?"

"I didn't know it was your bed," she blurted. "I

heard someone coming into the room and just wanted someplace to hide...." Too late she seemed to realize that she was only digging herself in deeper.

It was all appallingly clear to him now. He felt like the world's biggest fool. "So when I found you in my bed, you decided to distract me with sex."

Something painful twisted inside of him when she didn't deny it. He forced a smile to his stiff lips. "I have to admit you succeeded very well—almost well enough for me to consider letting you go."

He walked over to the telephone stand and picked up the receiver. "Sorry to disappoint you, but I'm not quite that stupid."

"Please," she said, moving close enough to grab his arm. "Don't."

He ignored her, wrenching out of her grasp. Her red cloak gaped open, giving him another glimpse of her sexy red bra and panties. The shape of her luscious body. A body he could envision with his eyes closed.

Another wave of disappointment washed over him as he punched out the phone number for the police. The greatest night of his life had been a lie. Her kisses. Her moans. Her unbridled passion. *All a lie.*

"I want to report a burglary," he said, when the operator came on the line.

"Wait, Michael," she implored. "Please. It's really

not what you think. I wasn't stealing the necklace—I was returning it."

Her words barely penetrated his brain. He was thinking about the days ahead. He'd have to press charges against her, tell the police what had happened between them. How he'd found her in his bed, made love to her. Perhaps even repeat his story in court. Every intimate detail of the night he'd spent with this woman. Hell, he'd even have to admit he'd been so dazzled by her that he didn't know her real name!

"Denver Police Department," barked a voice on the other end of the line.

Michael hesitated for a moment, then hung up the telephone. Maybe he should handle this on his own. Then another idea occurred to him, one so crazy he shouldn't even consider it. Yet the more he thought about it, the more it appealed to him.

When he turned to face her, Michael saw tears glimmering in her eyes. They almost looked authentic. Oh, yes, she was very good.

She might be just what he needed.

"So you were returning the diamond necklace to the safe?" he said, playing for time until he could decide exactly what he wanted to do with her. "I'm not sure I understand."

"I think you will when I tell you my name."

He waited, all too aware of her alluring vanilla

scent around him. On him. For the first time in his adult life, Michael wondered whether he had pleased her last night. Then he wondered why he cared.

"Am I supposed to guess?" he asked, growing even more irritated, especially when he remembered how anxious he'd been to learn her name after dancing with her at the masquerade ball. How concerned he'd been that he might never see her again. "Let's see...Lola? Jezebel? Delilah?"

His barbs brought a soft blush to her pale cheeks. "It's Sarah."

Sarah. A name as sweet and innocent as the woman he'd held in his arms last night. A name so at odds with the calculating thief Michael had found looting his safe this morning.

Lifting her chin, she slid off the mask covering her face. "Sarah Hewitt."

Hewitt. The name sounded vaguely familiar, but he couldn't quite place it. It didn't help that he found the sight of her lovely face—now completely exposed to his view—so distracting. "And?"

She seemed surprised that he didn't recognize her name. "My grandfather is Bertram Hewitt."

"And?" he prompted again, still clueless. Maybe she was trying to distract him with name games. If so, it wasn't going to work. However, the way her cloak kept gaping open did distract him.

She seemed too upset to notice that his gaze kept drifting downward. That he had a perfect view of her skimpy red panties. The smooth expanse of her flat stomach. The swell of her breasts in the lacy red bra.

Or maybe she knew exactly what she was doing. Maybe this was all part of her strategy. It sure as hell had worked for her last night. Michael forced his gaze up to her face, determined not to underestimate her again.

"My grandfather went into business with Seamus Wolff in 1950," she explained with a hint of exasperation. "Hewitt and Wolff Estate Brokers. Does that ring a bell?"

Now it clicked. "You're telling me you're related to that crazy old coot who broke into our house a few years ago?"

Her mouth thinned. "He's not crazy, just...bitter. He's lived a lifetime believing your grandfather cheated him. Only he doesn't have any way to prove it."

"Cheated him?" Michael echoed. "Unlike your family, Red, the Wolffs aren't thieves. We don't break into people's houses...or steal into their beds."

Her cheeks flamed. "I don't expect a man like you to understand, but..."

"A man like me," he interjected, taking another step closer to her. He knew people found his size intimidating. He wanted to throw her off balance, just as she'd done to him since their first kiss. "What exactly is that supposed to mean?"

She didn't back down. "You know very well what I mean." Emerald fire flashed in her eyes. "You're rich. Powerful. Ruthless."

"Is that all?" he challenged, inching closer. "How about passionate? Experienced? Satisfying?"

Michael didn't think it was possible for her blush to deepen. He was wrong. Through his anger, he wondered at the contradiction. A calculating thief. A blushing innocent. She played both roles so convincingly.

It made him think once again of the opportunity before him. *Dare he risk it?*

Sarah pulled the cloak tightly around her, as if suddenly aware of her indecent exposure. "Would it make you feel any better if I admit I made a mistake last night? A huge mistake. I'm sorry."

Her apology didn't make him feel a damn bit better. "I'm still waiting to hear why I shouldn't have you thrown behind bars for attempted burglary."

She met his gaze. "I realize you have no reason to believe anything I say, but I'm going to tell you the truth anyway, something I probably should have done the moment we met."

"I know how difficult it can be to break old habits."

She ignored his sarcasm. "I came here last night to return the diamond necklace. My grandfather stole it while your family was in Jamaica for Christmas. He's obsessed with it. Obsessed with a vendetta that he's carried with him for over fifty years."

"You're telling me an old man breached one of the best security systems around and I didn't even know it?"

"He may be old and bitter, but he's not dumb," Sarah replied. "He learned a lot of tricks in prison after he got convicted of stealing the necklace the first time. Tricks that he taught me. But I've never used them until now. I swear."

"Well, that's good enough for me," Michael said wryly.

"I'm here for his sake," she continued as if he hadn't spoken. "Because I can't stand the thought of him going to prison again. Because I love him." Her mouth trembled. "Maybe you can't understand that."

He did. Better than she knew. But he still wasn't convinced she was telling the truth. Old Bertram Hewitt was a known felon. Still...

"And just so we're clear," she said, squaring her shoulders, "if you do call the police, I won't tell them what I just told you. There's no proof, so it will be your word against mine. My grandfather is too old to go back to prison."

Michael gaped at her. "So you're willing to go to prison in his place?"

"I don't want to," she said, so softly he could barely hear her. "But I will."

Damn. Not only beautiful and cunning, but noble, too. He kept staring at her, wondering if he could believe her. Wondering if she knew how much he still wanted her.

That was the problem. Michael simply wasn't ready to let this woman go yet, thief or not. So why not take advantage of her unique talents? Both in bed and out.

Not that he'd ever force her into his bed. He wanted her to come willingly. To want him. Not his diamond necklace. Not his money.

Just him.

He let the silence grow between them, her anxiety apparent. When she grew so pale he feared she might faint, Michael finally spoke. "I won't call the police to report you or your grandfather." He saw the spark of hope flare in her eyes. "On one condition."

That hope instantly turned to wariness. "What kind of condition?"

Michael inhaled deeply, hoping he wasn't about to make the biggest mistake of his life. "My grandfather comes home from the hospital today. He will be practically bedridden for several weeks, recovering from a broken hip. You will hire on as his full-time caretaker."

Her brow furrowed. "Me?"

He nodded. "You will move in immediately."

"Live here?" she sputtered, obviously taken aback by the unexpected terms of his condition. "I don't understand. Why would you possibly want to hire me? I don't have any experience as a nurse."

"He doesn't need a nurse," Michael explained, "just someone he can yell at to bring him water and fluff his pillows."

Suspicion narrowed her eyes. "That's all you want me to do?"

"Actually, there is one more thing."

She tensed, as if waiting for a sexual proposition. He was tempted. Sarah Hewitt had slept with him to save her grandfather. Would she do the same to save herself? Would he want her to?

No. He wanted Sarah to come to him all on her own. Driven by desire, not desperation. By a hunger for him that was as strong as what he still felt for her. A hunger he was determined to satisfy so he could move on. Just like he always did.

"Well?" she prodded, impatience straining her voice.

Or maybe it was trepidation. The woman was completely in his power. A heady feeling, even for a man who was used to controlling a dynasty.

Michael walked past her to close the safe. "I want you to steal something for me."

"I...don't understand"

He turned around to face her. "I need a thief."

She slowly shook her head. "Why? You're already rich."

He smiled at her naïveté. As if money could solve all of life's problems. "The item I want you to steal has no monetary value. At least, not yet."

"I think you're purposely trying to confuse me."

"Then I'll make it very simple," he replied. "I want you to steal my grandfather's will. He changed it six weeks ago and left the bulk of his estate to his wife. If he dies, she'll inherit quite a large fortune."

"That seems only fair," Sarah replied, "since she is married to the man. Or are you upset that he didn't leave his estate to you instead?"

He shook his head. "His fortune is not the issue. I already have more money than I could ever possibly need."

"Then why do you care if he leaves everything to his wife?"

"Because I think she's trying to kill him."

SARAH STARED UP AT HIM, shocked at his blunt accusation. It almost made her forget her own precarious predicament. *"Kill him?* What proof do you have?"

"None," he replied. "Yet. That's why I need you—

to steal the will and buy me some time to find proof to convince my grandfather that his wife is very dangerous to his health."

The man was serious. Or seriously paranoid. Either way, his plan made no sense. Sarah gathered her scattered thoughts, hoping to make him see reason.

"Even if I agreed to steal the will," she began, "what good would it possibly do? Surely his lawyer has a copy on file."

"There is no copy," Michael countered. "It's a handwritten will. My grandfather's lawyer is vacationing in Europe and won't be back for another month. He's the only attorney Grandfather trusts, so until he returns there's only one copy—the one I want you to steal for me."

He seemed so sure of himself. And of her. Sarah didn't like being put in this position, but what choice did she have? It was agree to his terms or face possible arrest. Even jail time.

"Where is this will?" she asked, stalling. She'd never stolen anything in her life—except a few incredible hours in this man's bed. Now she was paying the price.

"My grandfather keeps it in a private safe in the bedroom he shares with Blair, his wife."

She shook her head, still seeing too many holes in his plan. "If I steal it, all he has to do is draw up a new will."

"Let me worry about that."

He'd apparently thought of everything. Rich. Powerful. Ruthless. A man who could do whatever he wanted. Even blackmail a woman after making love to her.

"Are you absolutely certain this new will even exists?" she persisted, still trying to find a way out. "Have you seen it?"

He gave a brisk nod, obviously growing impatient with all her questions. "I was one of the witnesses."

But Sarah wasn't ready to concede yet. He was asking her to commit a crime. And she simply didn't know the man well enough to know his true motives.

"Does your grandfather suspect her at all?"

"No. He's smitten." Michael's molten gaze spilled over her. "He obviously doesn't realize how deceptive a beautiful woman can be."

She wasn't going to apologize again. Michael had hardly been an innocent bystander last night. Just thinking about all the things he'd done to her made a heated flush crawl up her neck.

Sarah closed her eyes, well and truly caught in his lair. "And what if I don't like the terms of your condition?"

"You know the alternative."

She opened her eyes again, hearing something in his voice that seriously made her wonder if he was bluffing. A twinge of regret? Maybe even guilt? Neither one fit with his ruthless reputation. No doubt it was just wishful thinking on her part.

"So to keep you from calling the police," she began, wanting to make certain she understood him, "I must move into this house, care for your grandfather and steal his will."

"That's right. And I want you to leave the safe standing wide open, so Blair knows the will is gone. Otherwise, what's the point?"

"And if I'm caught?"

"We'll have to work together to make certain that doesn't happen."

Now she heard something else in his voice, something that told her he wanted more from her than the theft of his grandfather's will. She met his gaze, startled by how much it reminded her of a real wolf. Patient. Assessing. Fully aware of his prey.

Every instinct told her to run, that this man truly was dangerous. Because he could do more than take away her freedom. He could ravage her heart.

But only if she let him.

Michael Wolff might be rich and powerful and ruthless. He might even be passionate and experienced and satisfying. Very satisfying. But he didn't own her mind or her body. In fact, it might be extremely satisfying to show this wolf that he'd met his match.

"Well?" he prodded, wanting an answer.

"I'm considering your offer," she hedged, still weighing the risks. They were considerable on both sides. But then again, taking risks had been one of her New Year's resolutions.

"Just so we're perfectly clear about the terms of the agreement," he stated, fully in business mode now. "If you refuse my offer, then I call the police. If you tell anyone the real reason you're here, then I call the police. If anything happens to my grandfather while you're on duty, I call the police."

So much for the hope that he was bluffing. "Then you are blackmailing me."

"I'm giving you a gift," he countered. "Take it or leave it."

5

MICHAEL WISHED he didn't care so much about her answer.

Guilt seeped into his conscience at the trapped expression on her face.

A trap of her own making.

He couldn't forget that fact—especially when she looked up at him with shadows in those mossy green eyes, making him feel like the world's biggest bully.

He steeled himself against the remorse rising up in his throat. Tightly clenching his jaw to keep from saying the words he knew she wanted to hear. That he believed her story. That he'd forget he ever found her rifling through his safe. That he'd just let her go.

Not possible. Not after that incredible night they'd shared together. Sarah Hewitt had walked willingly into his lair, and now he intended to keep her here for a while.

For his grandfather's sake, he reminded himself.

"You don't leave me much choice," she said at last. "I'll take it."

He could finally breathe again. "Fine. I'll have one of the maids make up a room for you."

She gave a brisk nod. "I left my car parked down the mountain road about half a mile. I'll just drive back to my house and pack a couple of suitcases. Make a few arrangements. It should only take me a couple of hours."

He shook his head. "You're not allowed to leave this house without my permission."

"Not *allowed?*" Her delicate nostrils flared with indignation. "That's ridiculous! What about my clothes? My job..." Her mouth slammed shut and he could see the apprehension in her eyes.

Her behavior only piqued his curiosity more. "What job? Where do you work?"

She didn't say anything.

He was damn tired of this verbal tug-of-war between them. They'd been so in sync the night before, so perfect together, in every way.

"Fine," he clipped. "Don't tell me. I can hire a fleet of investigators who can obtain any information about you I desire."

Sarah met his gaze.

"I work as a teller at Consolidated Bank."

He nodded, surprised that he hadn't noticed her there before. Sarah Hewitt had obviously noticed him and decided he was an easy mark.

"Don't worry about your job," he assured her. "I'll talk to the bank president and make sure it's still waiting for you when you're through here."

She arched a brow. "It doesn't bother you to have a thief employed at your bank?"

"I thought you weren't a thief."

"I'm not. But if you believe that, then why don't you let me go?"

He shrugged. "I'm not sure I do believe it. Maybe you'll have the chance to prove it to me during your stay these next few weeks."

"By breaking into your grandfather's safe and stealing his will?" she asked wryly.

His gaze drifted to her full mouth. "Among other things."

She moved slightly away from him, as if suddenly disconcerted by his nearness. "What about clothes? I can't wear this cloak every day."

He waved away her concern. "I'll send one of the maids to your place. She can pack a couple of bags. Just make a list of whatever you think you might need."

She stared up at him. "Then I really am a prisoner here?"

"You're my guest," he countered, steeling himself against the despair in her voice. He couldn't forget the way she'd deceived him, or how easily he'd let her. "I think you'll find the accommodations much more comfortable here than the county jail."

She picked up the picnic basket. "I'd like to go to my room now."

"Of course," he agreed, reaching for the telephone. "I'm sure you're tired after last night."

He noticed every reference to the night they'd spent together unsettled her. Good. He didn't want to be the only one.

Michael dialed the housekeeper's number, then asked her to prepare a room immediately for his father's new caretaker. His staff was trained well enough not to ask questions, even at six o'clock in the morning.

When he hung up the receiver, he found Red in his bed again. Only she wasn't waiting there for another rendezvous with him. She was tearing the tangled silk sheets apart, searching for her skirt and blouse.

He liked her angry. It brought a heated flush to her cheeks and fiery sparks lit her green eyes.

Michael reached over and parted a canopy drape. "Can I be of service?"

Her gaze turned wary as she backed off the opposite side of the bed. "No, I already found them."

"Your room will be ready in a few minutes."

She clenched the clothes to her chest, as if half expecting him to rip them out of her arms and ravish her. "I'd like to get dressed now."

"Go right ahead."

"In private," she said between clenched teeth.

He thought about reminding her that he'd already seen her naked, but he'd pushed her far enough for one day. They both needed some time apart. Despite everything, he truly didn't want her to hate him.

"You may use my dressing room." He smiled. "But don't take too long or I might think you tried to climb out the window. We're on the third floor, so I wouldn't risk it anyway if I were you. It's quite a long fall."

Her expression told him leaping out the window might be preferable to spending any more time in his company.

She walked past him, then turned at the door of the dressing room. "How do I know you'll keep your word? What if I do everything you ask, but then you still turn me and my grandfather over to the police?"

He wondered why that possibility hadn't occurred to her before now. "I guess you'll just have to trust me."

She hesitated, then gave a slight nod, obviously aware that he hadn't left her with any other choice.

He had all the power.

Michael watched her disappear behind the dressing room door. He'd been such an idiot last night, not even questioning how she'd found her way into his locked bedroom. No doubt because all the blood in his brain had rushed south as soon as he'd seen her in his bed.

He couldn't remember the last time a woman had affected him this way. There was no denying the chemistry between them. But that was all there was to it. And one thing was for damn certain. He'd never let Sarah Hewitt fool him again.

SARAH LOOKED AROUND the opulent room that was to be her prison. It was called the Red Room, according to the maid who had led her here. The young Hispanic woman had left to fill the water pitcher, leaving Sarah time to contemplate her fate.

She walked over and perched on the edge of the brass bed, running one hand over the silky red coverlet. Had Michael been trying to send a message by placing her in here? Intimating that she was a harlot?

Sarah knew his opinion shouldn't matter. But it did. Last night had been special to her. Magical. Even the catastrophe of Michael catching her with her hand in his safe couldn't change that.

She walked over to the large round top window, impressed by the magnificent view of the snow-capped Rocky Mountains. How long would she have to stay here? Surely Michael would reconsider his demand that she steal the will. Once his anger cooled, he'd come to his senses.

"Settling in, I see."

She turned to see Michael framed in the doorway. He wore a bulky black turtleneck sweater and black denim jeans. He must have just come out of the shower because his dark hair was wet and slicked off his forehead.

"Do I have any choice?"

"No." He walked farther into the room, his gaze raking over the garish decor. "I thought this room would suit you."

She stared at him for a long moment, wondering why he was trying to bait her. He already had her right where he wanted. Then again, a man liked Michael probably enjoyed flexing his power.

What she needed was a can of wolf repellent. Industrial strength. Where was the man who had held her last night? Had made her lose all common sense when he kissed her? Sarah wondered now if it really had been just a fantasy.

"The room is fine," she said evenly.

He gave a slight nod, then his gaze moved slowly over her and, despite her anger, her body tingled with the memory of what his hands could do. The way his broad fingers had stroked her most sensitive spots, applying just the right amount of pressure. She swallowed hard and found herself looking up into his perceptive gray eyes.

A shadow in the doorway made them both turn.

"Ah, here's Maria," Michael said, as the petite maid bustled into the room. She was barely out of her teens, her dark hair pulled back into a neat ponytail. "She'll drive to your house and pick up whatever you need."

Sarah opened her mouth to offer to go with the maid, then closed it again, knowing it would be futile. "That's very kind of you, Maria. Thank you."

"You're welcome," Maria replied, casting a curious glance at her boss.

Sarah retrieved her basket off the floor. "Here is my house key. Now if you'll give me just a moment, I'll write down my address and make a list of what I need."

"Certainly," Maria replied.

"You may run into my grandfather while you're there," she warned, looking around the room for a pen and paper. Michael pulled them out of a drawer, anticipating her needs. Just like he'd done last night.

She saw Maria looking at her expectantly and realized she'd lost her train of thought.

"Your grandfather," Maria reminded her in a soft voice.

"Yes," she said, making a list of her meager wardrobe. Between saving for graduate school and maintaining her share of the household expenses, new clothes hadn't been in her budget for a very long time. "I'll call him and let him know you're coming. Please, whatever you do, don't mention the Wolffs."

Maria glanced at Michael, then nodded. "Very well."

"Here you go," she said at last, tearing off the top leaf of paper.

Maria's gaze scanned the list, then she looked up at Sarah. "Is that all?"

"I won't be staying long," Sarah replied, more to Michael than the maid.

"I think you're overestimating my grandfather's powers of recovery," Michael said, then lowered his voice. "You'll stay as long as you're needed."

As long as I need you. He didn't say the words, but she understood his meaning just the same.

"Wait a minute," Sarah exclaimed, as the maid moved toward the door. It was high time to show Michael Wolff he didn't call all the shots. "I just thought of one more thing."

Maria handed her the list and Sarah quickly jotted down another item. Then she gave it back to Maria.

The woman's brown eyes widened at the new addition, but she just nodded, a smile curving her mouth as she walked out of the bedroom.

"You seem to be adjusting to our arrangement quite well," Michael observed.

"I do what I have to do."

"So I noticed."

She turned toward the window so he couldn't see how his words affected her. She knew he had every reason to feel deceived. Telling him how special last night had been to her wouldn't make either of them feel better. "This is a gorgeous view."

"I agree."

The tone of his voice told her he wasn't talking about the mountains. She turned around, every nerve in her body on alert. "I could just walk out of here. You have no real proof against me or my grandfather."

He took a step closer to her, then pulled a small 8mm tape out of his pocket. "Actually, I do."

She stared at the tape, dread filling her. "What's that?"

"We have security cameras fixed on every safe in the house. This tape recorded a five-foot by five-foot view in front of the wall safe in my room from December twenty-eighth through January second."

And that meant both she and her grandfather had starring roles on that tape, something that could send them both to prison.

He picked up a videocassette adapter from the shelf under the television set and slipped in the tape. "We can both watch it right now if you'd like."

She shook her head. "I'll stay. I'll do whatever you ask." Too late she realized he might take her words the wrong way.

But Michael just turned toward the door, taking the tape with him. "I'm on my way to the hospital. My grandfather will be coming home late this afternoon. I'll introduce you to him and his wife tonight at dinner. I'll expect you downstairs at seven o'clock sharp."

"I look forward to meeting your grandfather," Sarah said and meant it. She'd heard so many stories about Seamus Wolff growing up, all of them negative, that he'd taken the image of a horrible monster in her mind. Maybe it would be good for her to see that he was just a harmless old man.

Michael started to leave, then turned at the door. "By the way, we always dress for dinner. Will that be a problem for you?"

She was almost tempted to show up at the table naked just to spite him. "I'm sure I can find something suitable to wear."

"Good. I'll see you tonight then."

He left before she could reply, closing the door behind him. She almost expected to hear a key turn in the lock. Instead all she heard was Michael's heavy footsteps echoing down the long marble hallway.

Sarah walked over to the door and locked it from the inside, not certain Michael would respect the privacy of his prisoner. Then she shed her cloak and the wrinkled clothes underneath, eager to take a long, hot bath.

But first she needed to call her grandfather.

She picked up the phone, then dialed the number

of the house they shared. After five rings, he answered.

"Hello?"

"Hi Grandpa, it's me."

"Hello, Sarah," he replied, relief in his voice. "Where are you? I've been worried."

"I should have called sooner." She took a deep breath. "I just wanted to let you know that I won't be home for a few days...maybe longer. I'm spending some time in the mountains with a...friend."

Sarah hated lying to her grandfather, but what choice did she have? If he knew she was trapped at the Wolffs'... She didn't even want to think about his reaction. Bertram's hatred ran so strong and deep that she couldn't be sure he wouldn't do something crazy.

"That's nice," Bertram replied. "But kind of sudden, isn't it?"

She gripped the phone more tightly in her hand. "One of my New Year's resolutions is to be more spontaneous." That much was true and she'd certainly fulfilled it last night. "Another friend plans to join us. She's going to stop by the house and pick up a few things for me. Her name is Maria."

"I'll look for her," he promised. "Have a wonderful time, honey. And don't you worry about me. I'll be just fine."

"I know you will," she replied. "If Mom and Dad

call tonight, please wish them a happy New Year for me and tell them I decided to take a vacation."

"They'll be glad to hear it," Bertram said. "We all think you work too hard."

Her parents phoned at least once a week from California and e-mailed her almost daily. She found herself wondering if e-mail was allowed in prison.

"Sarah?" Bertram said after a long stretch of silence. "You still there?"

"Yes, I'm here." She didn't want to hang up the phone, not certain when she'd see him again. Would it be days? Weeks? That incriminating tape put Michael firmly in control of her life.

"Don't forget to take your blood pressure pills," she reminded him.

"Every morning at breakfast," he assured her.

"You've got a dentist appointment next Tuesday." She twisted the phone cord around her fingers.

"It's on my calendar."

"If I'm not home by then I want you to call a taxi," she continued. "You know what happened last time you tried to drive."

"That wasn't my fault," Bertram countered. "There was a blind spot in my side mirror." He still bristled at the fact that his driver's license now restricted him to within five miles of his home. Another law he routinely broke.

"I know, but promise me anyway."

His low grumble came across the phone line, but at last he said, "I promise."

"Thank you, Grandpa."

"Like I said before," Bertram intoned, "don't worry about me. Just have a good time."

Somehow she didn't think that was going to happen. But no need to make him worry about her more than he already did. "I will, Grandpa. Talk to you soon."

"Bye, bye, honey."

She hung up the phone and for some ridiculous reason felt like bursting into tears. How did she ever get into this mess? And more important, how would she ever get out?

6

THAT EVENING, Michael sat at the mahogany dining room table, impatiently tapping his foot against the plush Persian rug on the floor. He'd made it perfectly clear that he expected Sarah at seven o'clock and she was already ten minutes late.

"Where the hell is dinner?" Seamus grumbled. "They near about starved me in that torture chamber they call a hospital."

"We're waiting for the new girl," Blair said, turning a page of the magazine in front of her. "Michael asked her to join us for dinner."

Seamus's scowl deepened as he turned to Michael. "What new girl? Since when did you start bringing your girlfriends home for dinner?"

"She's not my girlfriend," he replied, understanding now why the nurses had looked so relieved when he'd arrived to take Seamus home. "Her name is Sarah and she will be taking care of you until you're fully recovered."

For once he was glad his grandfather referred to his servants by their first names only. Usually Michael thought it incredibly arrogant, but he knew the name Hewitt would raise an alarm for his grandfather, even if Michael hadn't immediately recognized it himself.

"Well, if Sarah doesn't appear in the next thirty seconds," Seamus muttered, "she's fired."

As if on cue, Sarah walked into the dining room. She wore a black cocktail dress you could find on any department store rack. But the simplicity of it lent her an elegance he couldn't deny.

Her chestnut hair was swept up off her graceful neck into one of those complicated arrangements he never understood. Unlike Blair, she wore no jewelry except a tiny pair of pearl earrings.

Sarah smiled at everyone but him.

"Good evening," she said, moving toward the empty place setting.

Michael stood up and pulled out a chair for her. She hesitated, as if worried he might suddenly yank it out from underneath her. After a moment, she sat down.

Did Sarah really distrust him that much?

For some reason the thought disturbed him. Her attitude was hardly surprising, considering their arrangement—or rather, his arrangement. She was completely at his mercy.

Only he was the one suffering.

Like now, seeing the silky tendrils of her hair curling at the nape of her neck. He wanted to lift them away and kiss the smooth, creamy skin underneath. Inhale her sweet vanilla scent. Relive the fantasy.

Instead, he returned to his chair and said, "You're late."

"I must have lost track of time." Sarah picked up her white linen napkin and laid it across her lap.

Seamus snorted. "You and my wife should get along just fine."

"What?" Blair looked up from her magazine. "Did you say something, Seamus?"

"Time to eat," he clipped, as a maid brought out the first course.

For several minutes, the only sound in the dining room was spoons clinking against the china soup bowls. Michael found he didn't have much of an appetite. He'd rather watch Sarah than eat.

She didn't look up from her bowl until she'd scraped up the last drop of soup.

It suddenly occurred to him that she'd probably gone the entire day without eating. He'd made no arrangements for either breakfast or lunch for her. Had he become so vindictive that he'd literally starve a woman for damaging his ego?

Michael pushed his soup bowl away, feeling a little nauseous now. Perhaps he should let her go. Forget about the whole thing.

"So, girly," Seamus said, wincing as he shifted in

his chair, "what kind of experience do you have with grumpy old men?"

"You're not old, darling," Blair murmured, reaching out to pat his gnarly hand.

Seamus ignored her. "I'm still waiting for an answer, girly."

Sarah reached for a roll. "I'm still waiting for you to call me by my real name."

Seamus's brown eyes narrowed. "You're working in my house, eating my food, so I can call you anything the hell I want."

Michael leaned forward, ready to intervene. He might be angry with the woman, but that didn't mean he'd sit by and let his grandfather verbally abuse her.

But Sarah spoke before he had a chance. "As a matter of fact, Nappy, I've been taking care of my grandfather for quite a few years."

Seamus's eyes narrowed. "What did you call me?"

She looked up at him, her face as innocent as an angel. "I'm sorry, it just slipped out. You remind me so much of my cairn terrier, Nappy. That's short for Napoleon because he thinks he rules the world."

Michael tensed, waiting for his grandfather to explode for comparing him to a dog. Was Sarah purposely trying to antagonize the man? Get herself kicked out of here before she could fulfill her part of the agreement?

Seamus stared at her, his jaw working. Then he burst out laughing. "Nappy. I like it. And in my opinion, the world would be much better off if I did rule it."

A smile haunted her lips. "It seems you and your grandson have a lot in common."

"Score another point for the hired help," Seamus said, turning toward Michael. "Looks like neither one of us scare her a bit. But I'll still bet she won't last a week."

"I'll take that bet," Michael replied. "A hundred dollars says she stays a least two weeks."

He saw Sarah blanch and knew she didn't plan to stay here that long. But his grandfather actually liked her and he considered that a small miracle. Of course, he didn't know she was the granddaughter of Bertram Hewitt. And Michael had no intention of telling him.

"Only a hundred?" Seamus chuckled. "Not too sure of yourself, are you, boy?"

"Then let's make it a thousand," Michael offered.

"Now you're on," Seamus replied, leaning back in his chair as the maid set the entrée in front of him.

"A thousand dollars?" Sarah echoed, looking back and forth between the two of them. "You're wasting that much money on a silly bet?"

"That's one of the joys of the filthy rich," Seamus

told her. "We can waste our money on all kinds of silly things. Right, Blair?"

She looked up from her plate, obviously not following the conversation. "Right, darling." Then she reached over to pat her husband's hand again. "It's so good to have you home again, Seamus. We're going to have to take extra special care of you."

Seamus grunted as he tore a roll apart. "If you're so all fired anxious to take care of me, why did we have to hire Sarah?"

Good question. One that Blair didn't seem able to answer.

Michael shoved his guilt about blackmailing Sarah aside. He simply couldn't let anything interfere with making sure his grandfather was safe. Unfortunately, stealing that will seemed to be the only way to do it. If nothing else, it would buy him time until he found evidence that Seamus's wife wanted to become a widow, evidence that would finally convince his grandfather that the woman was no good.

"You know I would if I could," Blair finally replied. "But I've never been any good around invalids. Besides, we're about to start renovations on one of the attic rooms and I simply must sift through all the junk up there."

"Just toss it out," Seamus said. "There's nothing worth keeping."

Blair smiled. "You never know. Remember that

diamond necklace you found in one of those trunks from the Durham estate? It made you the man you are today."

Sarah dropped her fork, the silver clanking loudly against the china. "Excuse me," she murmured, not meeting Michael's gaze.

Perhaps she wasn't as cool and calm as she pretended. Michael would certainly love to see more of the emerald fire he'd seen before in those green eyes. He'd lost himself in the heat of her gaze, the heat of her body, last night.

"I'm ready for bed," Seamus announced abruptly, pushing his wheelchair away from the table.

Michael stood up. "I'll help you."

"No," Seamus countered. "I want Sarah to do it."

"DAMN, IT FEELS GOOD to be home," Seamus said, as Sarah pushed his wheelchair into the bedroom. "Those nurses got mighty prickly by the end of my stay."

"Imagine that," Sarah murmured under her breath.

Two of the male servants had carried him up the stairs to the third floor. After that experience, Seamus announced he wasn't coming down again until he could walk on his own two feet.

The sacrifice shouldn't be too much of a hardship, since his bedroom was almost the same size as her house. It was more a suite actually, one he shared with his wife. Only Blair hadn't come upstairs yet.

Sarah walked over to the hospital bed that had been delivered that afternoon. A pair of green-striped pajamas lay neatly folded on the end. The maid had turned down his bed, too. In fact, Maria had spent so much time preparing Seamus's room, Sarah had been forced to give up her plan to steal the will before dinner.

Not that Michael had supplied her with much information yet. She didn't know if the safe was in the wall or in the floor. If it was locked with a combination or a key. Or even if he'd dismantled this room's security camera yet.

Despite her anxiousness to leave, she couldn't take any chances. She had to plan this break-in very carefully. Seamus didn't strike her as a man who would overlook a theft, even one arranged by his grandson. He certainly hadn't shown any mercy to his former best friend.

"Do you need help undressing?" she asked, holding up the pajamas.

"Not since I was two years old," Seamus retorted, pain etching deep frown lines on his brow. "Sorry to disappoint you, Sarah, but this is one man you'll never see naked. If I do need any help with my clothes, I'll call my grandson."

She put down the pajamas. "Is there anything I can get you?"

"How about a bottle of bourbon?"

"Somehow I don't think your doctor would approve." She picked up the bottle of pain pills on his nightstand. "Especially while you're taking these."

He waved a hand in dismissal. "I don't need those anymore. Make me too woozy. A man's got to stay in control at all times."

Sarah rolled his wheelchair over to the bed, then helped as he hoisted himself onto the mattress. "Just one more reason not to drink bourbon."

"You're as bad as those nurses at that hospital...." His voice faded off as he stretched out on the bed and he suddenly looked every day of his seventy years. "Maybe I'll have one of those pills after all. I'm so damn tired. It's hell to be old."

She'd heard the exact same sentiment from her grandfather. "You'll feel better in the morning."

He scowled. "I really hate it when people say things like that."

She walked over to the nightstand and poured him a glass of water from the pitcher. Then she opened the pill bottle and tipped a small pink tablet onto her palm.

"Here you go," she said, handing the pill to him. "This should help you sleep."

He leaned up on his elbow and popped it in his

mouth. Then he chased the pill with a big gulp of water. "Not nearly as satisfying as bourbon."

She took the glass from him. "But just as effective."

His gaze fell on the green-striped pajamas that she'd laid back on the end of the bed. "Where the hell did those come from?"

"They look new."

"They look like a nightmare." He fell back against the pillow, then waved a hand toward his dresser. "Get me an old flannel nightshirt. It's in one of the drawers somewhere."

Sarah finally found it in the sixth drawer she looked in, the one on the very bottom. When she pulled the nightshirt out, a black and white picture fluttered to the floor.

A picture of her grandmother.

Sarah picked it up. Anna Hewitt stood smiling in front of a freshly painted sign that read, Hewitt & Wolff Estate Brokers. Sarah knew her grandmother had been a bookkeeper for the business, though she'd been Anna Pratt then.

Why did Seamus have a picture of her grandmother in his dresser drawer? Or was it simply a memento of the business he'd shared with her grandfather? Sarah turned to ask Seamus, but it was too late.

He was already sound asleep.

"MY GRANDFATHER likes you."

Sarah swallowed a gasp as she whirled to find Michael behind her in the darkened hallway. Had he been lying in wait for her?

She took a deep breath, her heart pounding. "He has a funny way of showing it."

"He's cautious," Michael replied. "He's been burned by women before."

"Maybe it has something to do with the way he treats them. You heard the way he talked to his wife at dinner tonight."

"They don't have the best relationship," he admitted. "All the more reason to believe she's trying to get rid of him."

"Have you always been this paranoid?"

He took a step closer to her. "Have you always been this beautiful?"

His question left her speechless.

Moonlight from the hall window cast shadows over his face, making it impossible to read his expression. But she could see the light, the hunger, shining in his eyes.

Sarah felt it too, pulsating between them. Erotic memories of the night before washed over her. She swallowed hard and resisted the urge to step into his arms.

What was it about this man that brought all these

desires to the surface? Or was it the full moon making her feel this way?

He took another step closer to her. "I need to apologize," he said, his warm breath caressing her cheek.

She blinked. That was the last thing she expected him to say.

"I forgot to tell the staff to prepare breakfast and lunch for you," he continued, regret in his eyes. "It was never my intention to starve you during your stay. You're free to visit the kitchen at any time and help yourself to whatever you wish. The same goes for the library and the rest of the house. As long as you don't leave the grounds."

"So you really do intend to keep me prisoner here?" She'd been hoping his apology would preclude a change of heart. Obviously, she was giving Michael Wolff too much credit. Despite her attraction to him, he was as obstinate as ever.

"You owe me, lady," he said huskily.

But for what? Breaking into his safe? Falling into his bed? Which act was the biggest crime in Michael's mind? Sarah wasn't sure she wanted to know.

"I don't like deceiving your grandfather," Sarah replied, "or his wife."

"But you had no problem deceiving me with your seduction."

She shook her head. "It's not what you think. I..."

Her voice trailed off. How could she possibly tell him the truth? He wouldn't believe her anyway.

She turned to go back to her room but he grasped her elbow to stop her.

"You what, Sarah? You *wanted* me to find you in my bed? You *wanted* to sleep with me?"

She fixed her gaze on the broad fingers clasped around her arm. She didn't dare let him look into her eyes, afraid he'd see the truth there.

"Last night was a mistake." She couldn't breathe properly when he stood this close to her. "A big mistake."

"I disagree," he said, drawing her against him. His lips skimmed the top of her head, causing a delicious shiver to ripple through her traitorous body.

She closed her eyes. "Let me go."

"There's one way to prove that you didn't mean to deceive me," he murmured, his fingers loosening their grip and slowly caressing her arm. "A way to prove that you're not a heartless liar."

She couldn't concentrate when he was touching her like this—his fingers skimming lightly across her skin. Up and down. Up and down.

His other arm curled around her shoulder, his hand sliding down the curve of her back. "One very simple way."

She forced herself to meet his gaze, her body

thrumming as his hand slid sensuously over the curve of her hip. "How?"

He pulled her closer, his mouth a hairbreadth from her own. "Come back to my bed tonight."

Desire warred with reason as his hands continued their slow, seductive assault on her body. His lips touched one corner of her mouth, then the other. A low moan escaped her throat.

Sleep with him. Just as she'd done last night. She could indulge in the temptation once more. Enjoy the thrills of this moonlight madness.

Yet morning would come again. Then what? If he let her go, she'd have sold her body for her freedom. If he kept her prisoner here, then that would make her little more than his sex slave.

Both of those possibilities brought a bitter taste to her mouth. She stepped away from him before he could sweeten his offer with a kiss—a kiss she knew would be hot enough to melt away all her reservations.

Sarah had to hold on to the one power she had left. The power to refuse him this.

"I think that would be another mistake." She pulled away from him, disappearing into her room before he could convince her to change her mind.

Sarah locked the door behind her, breathing hard as she slumped against it.

Some primitive part of her almost wished he'd

knock the door down. That he'd pursue her until her desire overcame her common sense—something she knew wouldn't take long. Not with a man as skilled at making love as Michael.

But the door stayed intact. The wolf had let her go. This time.

_____ 7 _____

MICHAEL SLOWLY AWOKE as something warm and wet lapped at his neck. He'd spent half the night tossing and turning, all too aware that Sarah lay sleeping in the next room. Naked and alone. Not that he knew she was naked. It was just that he kept picturing her that way in his mind.

Something whacked against Michael's face, bringing him to full conscience. He opened one eye to see a small dog staring at him. It barked once, its tail wagging.

Michael struggled to sit up. "What the hell?"

At the sound of his voice, the dog scampered off his bed and out of the room. He'd left the door ajar last night, hoping that Sarah would change her mind and slip into his bed.

Instead, some furry mutt had found his way into the house. And into his bedroom!

He threw back the covers and gave chase, spotting the dog right outside his door. He lunged for it and missed, knocking his shoulder against the wall.

The vibration shook a small pillar holding a seventeenth century vase. Michael reached out to steady the teetering vase, then turned to see the dog sitting in the middle of the hallway, watching him.

"Come here, mutt," he intoned, slowly approaching it.

The dog turned tail and scampered down to the other end of the hallway. Michael chased after it, wondering which one of the staff had brought this beast to work. Whoever it belonged to would find a spot in the unemployment line today.

The dog wove around Michael's legs, then headed in the opposite direction, thoroughly enjoying the game. When Michael stopped to catch his breath, the dog emitted three excited barks.

The door to Sarah's room swung open and she stepped out into the hallway wearing a long white flannel nightgown that brushed the tops of her bare feet. Delicate lace lined the cuffs at her wrist and the high button collar at her slender throat.

"Nappy," she scolded. "What are you doing out here?"

"This is your mutt?" Michael asked, breathless now for an entirely different reason.

Her dark hair hung loose and wild around her shoulders. Her cheeks glowed as pink as the tiny rosebuds embroidered on the bodice of the nightgown. But it was what lay beneath the virginal nightgown that most intrigued him.

He knew the shape of her breasts. The curve of her hips. Not to mention those incredible long legs. The way they'd wrapped around him two nights ago, pulling him closer...deeper....

"Meet Napoleon," Sarah said, breaking into his erotic reverie. She easily scooped the dog off the floor. "Nappy for short."

Michael started breathing again. "So what the hell is he doing here?"

"I had Maria bring him yesterday, along with the rest of my things. I couldn't just leave him in the house alone."

"Why can't your grandfather take care of him?"

"Because he can barely remember to take care of himself. And I don't want my grandfather trying to walk him on the icy sidewalks."

"Then put the dog in a kennel," Michael said, suddenly aware he was only wearing boxer shorts. Did that explain the rosy blush on her cheeks? "I'll pay for it."

She narrowed her green eyes. "Absolutely not."

Michael was all too aware of the way her gaze kept drifting south. So did most of the blood in his body. He turned and headed back to his room before she could see the effect she had on him. "That mutt is not staying here."

To his surprise, Sarah followed him into his bedroom.

"If Nappy goes," she exclaimed, "so do I."

Michael hastily pulled on his robe, cinching the silk belt around his waist. It was a silly argument—Michael didn't like dogs. Not since he was nine years old. A time and a memory he thought he'd put long behind him.

He turned to face her. "This is not negotiable."

"And this isn't one of your business deals," she countered. "Don't you understand? Nappy is part of my family. I'm not going to put him in some strange kennel, or abandon him to fend for himself."

Her green eyes sparkled in the morning sunlight and her cheeks were now flushed with righteous indignation. She obviously loved the little mutt.

For a brief moment Michael wondered what it would be like to be on the receiving end of that much devotion. To have a woman fight to keep him.

What Sarah didn't seem to understand was that he was the one calling the shots.

He folded his arms across his chest. "The dog goes."

"Then so do I."

Hell. She was calling his bluff over a damn dog. His jaw clenched as he weighed his options. If he got rid of the dog, she'd be gone, too. He'd either have to turn her into the police or forget about her. Something told him he wouldn't be able to do either.

Besides, he needed her to break into that safe and

steal the will for him. His grandfather's life depended on it.

"Please, Michael," she implored, laying her hand on his forearm, obviously sensing his weakness. Or maybe she knew he couldn't resist her when she touched him like that.

"All right," he conceded, swallowing his pride. "The mutt can stay."

Sarah's smile made his heart flip-flop. "Thank you, Michael."

"On a few conditions."

Her smile wavered. "Such as?"

"He stays completely out of my way. No more morning wake-up calls."

Amusement danced in her eyes. "You got it."

"And I don't want to hear him barking all day and night."

"He only barks when he gets excited," she assured him. "Or if there's an intruder. He's very protective."

Nappy didn't impress him as much of a guard dog. "He's restricted to the first floor and can sleep in the sunroom. I don't think he can cause much harm there."

"He's a cairn terrier," she reminded him. "Not a pit bull."

"And if he makes even one mess on the floor," Michael continued as if she hadn't spoken, "he's banished to the gardener's shed outside."

When Sarah started to protest, he held up one hand. "The shed is heated in the winter. The mutt won't freeze to death."

"I'm sure he'll be fine on the first floor. Nappy is very well trained." She nuzzled the dog against her cheek. "He won't be any problem. You'll see."

In Michael's opinion, the mutt was already a problem. He'd lost a battle with Sarah, and Michael didn't like to lose.

He didn't like dogs much either. But it looked as if he was going to have to tolerate this one, at least for a little while.

Michael sighed. "Just keep him out of my way."

Sarah walked out the open door, glancing over her shoulder. "You won't regret it."

He already did.

LATER THAT AFTERNOON, Sarah found herself summoned to Blair's private parlor. She sat on a wicker love seat while Blair reclined on a chaise lounge near the window, occasionally letting her gaze wander over the grounds.

"I thought it was time we got to know each other a little better," Seamus's wife said. "After all, you are taking care of my husband."

Sarah breathed a silent sigh of relief. She'd assumed Blair had heard about Napoleon and was as eager to get rid of her dog as Michael. But it seemed Nappy was safe for now.

"What would you like to know?"

Blair picked up a wineglass off the table next to her. "Everything."

Sarah knew that was impossible, not without revealing the real reason she was here. So she decided to stick with the boring stuff. "I was born and raised in Denver. I attended high school here, then went to the University of Colorado in Boulder. I've been accepted to graduate school, so now I'm trying to earn enough money to go."

"How fortunate for us that you were still available. I assume you have excellent references?"

"You can check with Michael," Sarah hedged. "He seemed perfectly happy with my qualifications."

"I'm sure that's not necessary," Blair replied, "especially as my Seamus seems so fond of you. Tell me, Sarah, have you ever been married?"

"No."

"It's wonderful when you find the right man," Blair mused. "I knew Seamus was the right man for me the moment I set eyes on him."

According to Michael, she'd fallen in love with his money. Then again, he was hardly the best judge of people. He still believed Sarah was a thief.

"How did the two of you meet?" Sarah asked,

truly interested. She'd heard about Seamus Wolff from her grandfather, but his bitterness had colored every story. He'd described his old business partner as a heartless predator. Yet she'd already seen some glimpses of humanity beneath Seamus's crusty exterior.

Now she found herself wondering the same about Michael. Was he really as ruthless as his reputation? Of course, she only had to look as far as her current predicament for the answer to that question.

"I used to be a hand model," Seamus's wife replied, holding one hand up to the window and admiring it in the sunlight. "Seamus owns a chain of jewelry stores and held a contest for the perfect hand to wear the perfect gem—an emerald he'd bought through an exclusive auction in South America."

"And you won?" Sarah ventured.

"Yes," Blair replied with a satisfied sigh. "I won."

Sarah sensed she was talking about more than the contest. "So do you still go out on modeling jobs?"

"Of course not," she said, taking another sip of her wine. "I'd rather stay home with my husband, in case he needs me."

Yet she couldn't, or wouldn't, run the simple errands that Sarah had been hired to do. Was that Blair's choice or did Seamus call all the shots in their marriage? Was the quest for power a hereditary trait in the Wolff family?

"So how exactly did Seamus break his hip?" Sarah asked, her curiosity getting the better of her. Michael had insinuated that suspicious circumstances surrounded the incident, but no one else had ever mentioned it.

"A car accident." Blair twisted her wedding ring around her finger. "A faulty brake line. A mountain road. Seamus could have been killed."

A chill went through Sarah as she listened. The woman had absolutely no emotion in her voice. When Blair dabbed her dry eyes, Sarah understood for the first time why Michael suspected her of foul play. Blair might be a wonderful hand model but she was a lousy actress.

"The doctor said Seamus was lucky he didn't break his neck," Blair continued with an unconvincing sniff. "Having come so close to losing him, I'm going to keep a very close eye on him from now on. A very close eye."

Sarah blinked at the sudden change of tone in her voice, one that could almost be called a warning. Did Blair actually believe she'd try to seduce a married man right under his wife's nose? A man old enough to be her grandfather?

Then again, he was old enough to be Blair's grandfather, too.

"I'm sure Seamus will appreciate that," Sarah answered, though she'd already learned the old man hated anyone fussing over him.

"Of course, I'm quite busy supervising all the renovations and clearing out the north attic room." She tipped up her wineglass and drained it, then fixed her keen blue gaze on Sarah once more. "But I will certainly pop in from time to time during the day to check on him."

Sarah nodded, wondering if she should bother to assure the woman that she had no intention of stealing her husband. Now, her husband's will was another matter.

Blair placed her empty wineglass on the table. "By the way, there will be several guests arriving Saturday night for a dinner party. We'll be celebrating Michael's birthday, so even Seamus will come downstairs for the event, which means you can have the night off."

It also meant his room would be empty, so she'd finally have access to the safe. "I'll look forward to it."

"Good." Blair smiled. "I'm so glad we've had this chance to talk, Sarah. Michael doesn't always have the best judgment where women are concerned, but I think you'll fit in just fine."

It seemed Seamus had the same judgment as his grandson. Blair didn't love him. It made Sarah both sad and suspicious. "Will that be all?"

She nodded. "You may return to your duties."

Duly dismissed, Sarah turned and walked out the door. No wonder Seamus was so cranky all the time. How could he stand living with her, even if she was young and beautiful?

And why did Sarah care? Her own grandfather would be thrilled about the dysfunctional Wolff family. He'd say Seamus deserved no better.

But everyone deserved love, and this ornate mansion seemed sadly devoid of it, except for the fierce devotion Michael had for his grandfather. And even that was tainted by Michael's suspicions about Seamus's wife. If Seamus ever discovered his grandson's plan to steal the will and prove Blair guilty, would he ever forgive him? Even if Michael was right?

"It doesn't matter," she muttered to herself as she headed downstairs to take Napoleon for a walk. "By then I'll be long gone."

MICHAEL SAT in his office on the top floor of the Consolidated Bank building, looking at Sarah Hewitt's personnel file. He'd had it sent up from the human resources department after explaining to the manager there that she'd be taking a temporary leave of absence.

No doubt the bank employees were already buzzing about her mysterious disappearance. Well, let them speculate. He didn't owe anyone any answers.

His gaze moved to the vital statistics kept on each employee. Age: twenty-six. Marital status: single. That didn't surprise him, since Sarah didn't seem like the cheating type. Rather funny, when you thought about it, since she was an aspiring thief.

In his heart, though, he wanted to believe her story. Wanted to believe it so much that he hadn't even watched that security tape, afraid that it would prove him wrong.

A knock on the door made him close the file before he said, "Come in."

Cole Rafferty walked inside. A former fraternity brother at Washington University, Cole now owned and operated one of the top security firms in Denver. He didn't do much fieldwork anymore, but for this job Michael wanted the best.

"Glad you could make it on such short notice," Michael said, standing up to shake his friend's hand.

"Hey, when the great and powerful Michael Wolff calls, I come running." Cole grinned. "Unless, of course, he's calling from the Chapel of Love in Reno, telling me to hop on a plane because he's about to marry a showgirl named Kiki and needs a best man."

Michael grimaced. "You'll never let me live that down, will you?"

"I bet Kiki still hasn't forgiven me for talking you out of it."

"I was young and stupid."

"And drunk as hell."

Michael laughed. "That, too."

"So what's up?" Cole asked.

"I need you to get rid of another gold digger."

Cole arched a brow. "You proposed to another Kiki?"

"Not for me. For my grandfather. I think his wife is trying to kill him."

Cole stared at him for a long moment. "That's a serious charge, Michael. Do you have any proof?"

"Not yet. That's why I called you. Solid proof is the only way I can convince him that his marriage is dangerous for his health."

Cole gave a slow nod. "So where do I start?"

"Check into Blair's background. Her maiden name is Ballingham. See if there are any previous marriages. Even a criminal record."

"Didn't your grandfather already do a background check? I thought that was his standard MO before matrimony."

Michael snorted. "Not with Blair. It was love at first sight."

"I take it you're not a believer in that phenomenon."

Michael shook his head, even as a vision of Sarah

in that white flannel nightgown flashed through his mind. "I literally can't afford to be."

"Good thing I'm not as rich as you," Cole replied. "Life wouldn't be near as much fun."

"If you find the evidence I need against Blair, I'll pay you a fee large enough to have all the fun you want."

"That's my kind of client," Cole quipped. "Anything else I can do for you?"

"We're having a small dinner party Saturday night. Just a few friends and business associates. You and Annie are invited."

Cole grinned. "I really hope we won't be able to make it. She's already a week overdue."

Michael could see the pride of impending fatherhood in Cole's eyes and felt something oddly like envy. He'd given up dreaming about a family of his own a long time ago.

"Then maybe you'd better not take a chance traveling up those mountain roads," Michael suggested.

"You're probably right." Cole stood up to take his leave. "So I'll have to make it up to you by finding the perfect birthday gift. Do you prefer a blonde or a redhead this year?"

Michael shook his head. "Thanks, but I've already got a date for the party. She's a brunette I met on New Year's Eve...."

Cole's cell phone chirped. "Hold that thought," he

said, pulling it out of his pocket. His eyes widened and he nodded, then hung up the phone.

"It's time."

"Annie?"

"I'm supposed to meet her at the hospital." Cole turned toward the door, almost tripping over his own feet.

"I'll drive you," Michael offered, pulling his car keys out of his pocket as he rounded the desk.

"I can drive."

"You can barely walk."

"I'm about to become a father." Cole grinned, then slapped his friend on the back. "Thanks, Wolff. I'll do the same for you someday."

But Michael knew that day would never come.

8

SARAH STOOD in the gallery of the Wolff mansion, staring up into a pair of mischievous gray eyes that reminded her of Michael's. The brass plate on the portrait read Colin David Wolff.

Michael's father.

It had been painted when he was a young man, younger than Michael was now. His wavy dark hair hung almost to his shoulders and his mouth was curved into a mocking smile, as if he thought posing for a portrait was a silly, but necessary, duty.

There was arrogance in the arch of his brow. Confidence in the set of his broad shoulders. A take-on-the-world attitude afforded to the very daring and the very rich.

In the short time she'd spent with Seamus Wolff, it sounded as if his son Colin had been both. She'd already heard how Colin had obtained his pilot's license when he was only sixteen, how he'd flown all over the world...until that fateful day seventeen years ago when his twin engine Cessna had gone down just outside of Vail.

As Sarah looked up into Colin Wolff's young face, she wondered if his last thoughts had been about the thirteen-year-old son he'd left behind. How much of what happened then had made Michael the man he was now?

"Here you are."

She turned to see Michael walking toward her. Sarah's heart contracted for the young boy he had been. "You were looking for me."

"Everywhere," he replied, his tone a mixture of exasperation and relief. "I expected you to be in my grandfather's room."

"He kicked me out," she explained. "Told me he wanted to take a nap and didn't need an overpaid baby-sitter to do it."

Michael's gaze moved to the portrait of his father. "I see you're becoming acquainted with the rest of the Wolff family."

She nodded. "I love to look at family portraits."

"Seamus had most of the earlier generations painted from old family photographs. Except for my favorite. Great-great-grandpa Jonah Wolff." He nodded toward a portrait on the wall a few feet away. "He came to Colorado for the gold rush and ended up opening a bordello with the prettiest women in the territory."

"How did Mrs. Jonah Wolff feel about that?"

He smiled. "She was one of the women. But she retired after the wedding."

"I have to see her portrait," Sarah said, heading down the row of pictures.

Michael walked with her. "She's right next to Jonah. Bridget O'Feeny Wolff."

Sarah looked up at the portrait of a dark-eyed young girl with very familiar gray eyes and a winning smile. "She is beautiful."

"Smart, too," Michael replied. "She turned the bordello into an exclusive men's club and charged an outrageous membership fee—which just made people all the more eager to join."

Sarah looked up and down the long row of family portraits. "I don't see a picture of your mother."

"That's because there isn't one." Michael turned and began walking briskly toward the end of the gallery.

Sarah followed him, aware that she'd obviously brought up a sore subject. His attitude only made her more curious. Now that she thought about it, Seamus rarely mentioned Colin's wife in any of his stories about his son. Had she died in the plane crash, too?

"I want to show you the new Egyptian collection Blair just acquired." Michael walked through another door. "Despite everything, I have to admit the woman has good taste."

Sarah followed him into another gallery. This one was smaller, the art displayed on marble pedestals and in several glass cases.

"What do you think?" he asked, after she'd perused the room.

"Very nice." Then she looked up at him. "Though I'm certainly no expert in Egyptian art."

"Neither am I." He stepped closer to her. "But I know what I like...and I know what I want."

She knew they weren't talking about art anymore. He wanted *her*. She saw the flash of heat in his gray eyes when he looked at her. Saw the way his gaze drifted to her mouth.

Before she could react, he drew her into his arms and kissed her. His mouth molding to hers, a low groan rumbling in his chest. Sarah heard herself moan in response as she sank against his hard body. His tongue stalked her lips until she opened for him, her mind racing as fast as her heart.

The next moment, he stopped, holding her at arm's length, his eyes now molten with passion. "Admit it, Sarah. You want me. As much as I want you."

Heaven help her, she did. Her body ached for his touch. For the way his gentle, skilled hands could bring her to the brink of ecstasy and back again. Holding her safe in his arms all the while.

Only that safety was an illusion. Michael Wolff

was more dangerous to her heart and her soul than any man had ever been.

His desire for her was palpable. But he didn't push her. He just waited, like a wolf assessing his prey— which just made him all the more dangerous in her eyes.

"Why were you looking for me?" she asked a little breathlessly, desperate to diffuse the tension now crackling between them.

He didn't seem to mind the sudden change of subject. "I want to invite you to my birthday dinner. As my date."

"I don't think that's a good idea." After what had just happened between them, she was certain of it.

"I think it's a wonderful idea," he countered. "It will give you the perfect alibi when you steal my grandfather's will."

The will. She'd almost forgotten about it. Not a mistake she could afford to make. Michael's interest in her was purely selfish. He wanted her. He wanted the will. He'd obviously take both, though, if given the chance.

"The dinner party is Saturday night," he continued. "There will be ten guests and my grandfather has already declared that he will come downstairs for the occasion. That means his room will be empty."

She nodded, her head whirling. Once she stole the

will for him, she could leave this house. Relinquish the hold he had on her. Both physical and emotional.

"But if I'm your date, when will I have time to steal the will?"

"I'll invite our guests to take a tour of the gallery after dinner," he explained. "I have several new acquisitions, including the Egyptian collection. Since the gallery is composed of several rooms, we'll all eventually become separated."

"So that's when I sneak away?"

He nodded. "I will, too, so if anyone does notice that you're missing, they'll assume I wanted some private time with my date, as I have in the past."

She couldn't let herself forget Michael's vast experience with women. His pursuit of her was nothing more than a game. One that he'd played many times before.

And that meant she had to ignore all the deeper feelings currently twisting around inside of her. Ignore the empathy for him that would creep in at the most unexpected times.

It was almost as if she had Stockholm Syndrome, where people held for ransom began to sympathize with their kidnappers.

Only Michael wasn't holding her hostage, not in the legal sense. And she certainly wasn't totally blameless for finding herself in this predicament. It had been her choice to crash the party and break into his safe. Her choice to sleep with him.

Her choice to walk into the lair of the wolf.

But if she wanted to walk out with her heart intact, she had to resist the temptation that he offered. Resist every touch. Every kiss. Every fantasy that kept her awake at night.

So dating him, even on pretense, was not a good idea. She just needed time to think of a better one. If she could just find an excuse to leave the mansion, even for a little while, it might help to clear her head. "I don't have anything suitable to wear."

"I'll take care of everything," he promised, giving her no way out. "Just be ready to come downstairs at seven o'clock on Saturday night."

She nodded, telling herself this was the best opportunity, perhaps the only opportunity to get access to Seamus's safe. Once she did, Michael would finally have to let her go.

"What do you think of Blair?" he asked, as they walked back into the main gallery.

"I didn't like her at first. But now I just feel sorry for her."

His step faltered. "You're kidding?"

She looked up at him. "No, I'm not. I think she's one of the most insecure women I've ever met."

He shook his head. "Then you don't know her very well."

"I had tea with her this afternoon," Sarah replied. "She seems very...lonely. I suppose it's easy to feel lost in such a big house, around such big, powerful men."

"Do you feel lost?" he asked softly.

Sarah looked into his eyes, wondering what he'd say if she admitted the truth. That she'd found herself, her center and her passion, the night they'd spent together. That he'd filled a void in her life she'd never noticed before, a void she could never ignore again.

"No," she said at last. "Do you?"

He stared at her for a long moment, then turned away and started walking for the door. "My grandfather's probably woken from his nap now."

Sarah followed him, wondering if he always ignored subjects that made him uncomfortable. When they passed the portrait of his father, she thought of another question.

"How did your mother die?"

Michael turned at the doorway. "What makes you think she's dead?"

Sarah stared at him, remembering the way Seamus had spoken of her in the past tense. "She's alive?"

A muscle flexed in his square jaw. "I honestly don't know. She left when I was nine." Then he turned and walked away.

Sarah stood alone in the cavernous gallery, thinking of her own family. Her parents and grandparents. They'd all lived crowded together in the same small house. Dependent on one another. Mostly happy. Love guiding them all the way. Even if that love sometimes went too far—as in the case of her grandfather.

She remembered her grandmother's funeral. How her grandfather had broken down and wept. How empty and quiet the house had seemed for months afterward. How much Sarah still missed her, even after all these years.

Despite everything, she wouldn't change her family for the world.

While Michael, the man who seemed to have everything, had lost his father and his mother. No wonder control was so important to him. He'd had so little of it as a child.

He was making up for it now. That's why he was trying to nail Blair for attempted murder. And why he was even willing to burglarize his grandfather's safe to prove it.

She just hoped he didn't lose what little family he had left in the process.

ON SATURDAY EVENING, Sarah walked into her room and found an evening gown laid out on her bed, along with whisper-thin silk lingerie and a pair of strappy heels.

The gown was magnificent. White gossamer that hugged her torso as if it had been custom-made for her. As if Michael had memorized every inch of her body.

Just as she'd done with him.

After donning the gown, Sarah stood in front of the dressing room's three-way mirror, still trying to believe the woman in the reflection was her.

The gown dipped low in the back, almost to her waist. Tiny crystals hand-sewn on the opaque fabric made it glimmer in the light.

She'd swept her hair off her neck, weaving it into a French braid. Then she twisted it into a knot, securing it with bobby pins. Tiny wisps of hair escaped, curling around her cheeks and the nape of her neck.

Taking a slow turn, Sarah looked at the dress from every angle.

In twenty-six years, she'd never worn anything this perfect, this expensive. It made her realize how seductive money could be. Slipping on the shoes, also a perfect fit, Sarah reminded herself this was just another fairy tale. Only this time instead of Red Riding Hood, she was Cinderella.

A fairy tale that would come to a not-so-happy ending when she broke into Seamus Wolff's private safe and stole his will. Then she'd be gone, leaving both the gown and Michael behind her forever.

A knock at the door brought her out of the dressing room. "Come in."

Michael entered, wearing a black tuxedo. Her heart skittered at the sight of him and she had to take a deep breath to collect herself. Oh yes, it was a good thing she was leaving after tonight. A very good thing.

"You look..." His voice trailed off in wonder as his gaze moved slowly over her.

She smiled. "So do you."

He took a step closer to her. "There's just one thing missing."

She watched him remove a familiar blue velvet case from his pocket. He flipped open the lid and she saw the diamond necklace nestled inside.

Sarah shook her head, almost afraid to touch it. That necklace had brought her here. Into this house. Into his bed. She feared if she put it on she might lose what little control she had left.

"Please," he said, seeing her resistance. "For my birthday."

She should have refused him, but when he said those words she thought of the boy who had spent so many birthdays without his parents. Was he really asking so much?

Without a word, she turned around so he could

put it on her. The necklace circled her throat and she reached up to smooth her fingers over the perfect gems.

Michael stood close behind her, working the clasp, his warm breath caressing her neck.

Sarah's skin tingled as his fingers brushed against her skin. "Having trouble?" she asked, a little breathless.

"The clasp is a little tricky," he replied. "It's so old, I'm afraid it will break if I force it."

As he leaned closer, she closed her eyes, inhaling his spicy, masculine scent. At last the clasp connected, but Michael didn't move away from her.

He carefully swept the wisps of her hair out from under the necklace. His hands slid over her bare shoulders, then he turned her to face him.

Awareness pulsed inside of her. "We should go downstairs."

"We should," he agreed, but still didn't move. "You are so damn beautiful," he murmured, his finger tracing over the curve of her cheek. "You should wear diamonds every day."

The drumbeat of desire pounded at every pulse point. "I don't think that's quite within my budget."

He gave a slight nod, then seemed to collect himself and held out his arm. "Are you ready?"

A loaded question. Ready to meet his guests? Or steal the will? Or fall into his arms? The answer was yes on all counts. But instead of telling him, she simply took his proffered arm and headed for the door.

One more night in the Wolff's lair. Then she would be free.

9

MICHAEL WATCHED Sarah from across the room, wondering how the men surrounding him could keep from doing the same. They were all smoking after-dinner cigars and congratulating Michael on his most recent business acquisition.

Seamus sat in his wheelchair, nursing a brandy. He didn't seem to be interested in the conversation either.

He followed his grandfather's gaze and saw Blair talking to a man half his grandfather's age. He'd never seen her so animated.

She certainly didn't look insecure to Michael. Or lonely.

Michael took a long sip of his brandy. The sooner he exposed Blair, the sooner he could concentrate on his own life. He'd been feeling dissatisfied lately. Restless. Corporate takeovers and buyouts no longer gave him the heady thrill of power they once had.

Michael stubbed out his half-smoked cigar, his gaze moving to Sarah once again. She'd been quiet during dinner, though he'd done his best to set her at ease.

She was so damn beautiful.

He wished he could celebrate his birthday with her alone. A private dinner. Dancing. One smile from her would be the perfect birthday gift.

But she wasn't smiling now. She looked tense, nervous. No doubt thinking about the crime that lay ahead—a crime he was forcing her to commit.

"Michael!"

He blinked, then turned to see his grandfather scowling at him. "Did you say something?"

"Hell, boy, you're only thirty years old, too young to lose your hearing yet."

The other men laughed indulgently. Michael joined them, shoving away any second thoughts. His grandfather's life was at stake. He'd do whatever was necessary to protect him.

"I need another brandy," Seamus informed him, holding up his empty glass.

"Sorry," Michael replied, shaking his head, "you're on pain medication. The doctor said to limit you to one glass."

"Now you sound just like my nursemaid." Seamus nodded in Sarah's direction. The rest of the group now turned their attention toward her.

One of them whistled low. "Damn, Michael, I could use a nursemaid myself. Where did you find her?"

In his bed. In his safe. Circling his heart. None of

which he was about to admit. "You know I never reveal my sources, gentlemen."

Seamus looked up at him. "Hell, he hasn't even told his own grandfather he's dating her."

Michael smiled. "You know I never kiss and tell."

Everyone laughed and he saw Sarah turn to look at him. The diamonds sparkled at her slender neck, reminding him of why she was here in the first place.

Seamus narrowed his gaze on her. "That necklace she's wearing looks damn familiar."

"I thought it would be perfect with her dress." Michael tried to sound nonchalant, but both he and his grandfather knew this was the first time he'd ever lent the family jewels to one of his dates.

"Perfect is the word for her," one of the other men murmured.

Michael drained his own glass of brandy, then rose to his feet.

"Shall we all take a tour of the gallery?"

It was time to make their move.

SARAH TRIED to make small talk with the woman beside her as they mounted the stairs to the second floor. But her mind kept drifting to what lay ahead of her.

Once they reached the gallery, she had to sneak away from the group, crack a safe, then slip back into the gallery before anyone noticed her missing.

Michael had made it sound so easy, but she wasn't as confident in her cat-burglar abilities. If someone saw her... No, she couldn't think that way. She just had to take it one step at a time.

"He's lethal, isn't he?" said the woman beside her.

Sarah glanced at her, remembering now that her name was Maureen. One of the young, blond wives in abundance here tonight. The vast age difference in the married couples had startled her. She'd heard of trophy wives, but never seen so many gathered together in one room before.

"Who?" she asked, her hand sliding along the polished mahogany banister.

"Michael, of course." Maureen leaned over the banister to watch him wheel Seamus to the back staircase, where a makeshift ramp had recently been installed.

"I'm not sure what you mean," Sarah hedged.

Maureen emitted an unladylike snort. She'd been drowning herself in cosmopolitans all evening. "I mean Michael Wolff is not only rich and powerful, but so very, very sexy." She slanted a weary glance at her stocky middle-aged husband. "A truly rare combination."

"The gallery is this way," Sarah informed her as they reached the top of the stairs.

Maureen followed her down the marble tile.

"That's why women can't stay away from Michael, even though he's cold as hell."

Just the opposite, Sarah thought, growing more irritated by the moment. He generated so much heat that she was almost ready to believe a person could spontaneously combust from it.

They entered the gallery and a few moments later Sarah saw Michael wheel his grandfather over to Blair. Then he turned and headed straight for her.

"Great sex," Maureen continued, oblivious to Michael walking up behind her, "and riches galore. What woman can resist?"

"I can," Sarah said softly, aware that Michael had heard every word.

Maureen turned and had the grace to blush. "Happy birthday, Michael."

"Thanks, Mo. I think Dick is looking for you."

Maureen grimaced. "Duty calls."

Sarah watched her walk away, not surprised that Michael was still single if that was the type of woman he socialized with. She'd caught more than one woman here tonight staring hungrily at him, like vultures, circling for fresh meat.

"It looks like the Egyptian collection is a big hit," he mused, as most of the guests began to migrate into the adjoining room.

"It should be donated to a museum someday," she said, "so more people can enjoy it."

Seamus rolled up to them. "Don't be giving him any more ideas. The boy already plans to fritter away everything he owns."

"Leaving my estate to a charitable foundation is not frittering it away," Michael replied.

"What foundation?" Sarah asked, surprised. But then, she knew Michael spurned the idea of marriage. So what else would he do with his fortune?

He shrugged. "I still need to do some research to make sure I pick a good one. Since I'm only thirty, I don't feel there's a rush."

"Just as well I'm leaving everything to Blair then," Seamus muttered, wheeling away from them. "At least I can be sure she'll spend it."

When they were alone, Michael turned to her. "Are you ready?"

She met his gaze. "If you're still certain you want me to do this."

He hesitated, his gaze following his grandfather. "I don't think I have any choice."

She knew he truly believed that. Just one more reason why any relationship with Michael Wolff was doomed. She didn't want to end up like Blair—the object of scorn and suspicion—or even worse, find herself replaced by someone like Maureen.

And that meant Sarah didn't have any choice either. "Let's do it."

Michael led her toward a private alcove. She saw a

few furtive smiles directed their way, but most of the people gathered there didn't pay them any attention.

A moment later, they were out of sight from the rest of the guests.

"Go through that door and you'll find the servants' staircase." He checked his watch. "If you're not back in fifteen minutes, I'll come looking for you."

She knew he meant to reassure her, but setting a time limit only made her more nervous. Fifteen minutes to commit a felony. Given how badly she'd bungled the last one, Sarah knew she didn't have a second to waste.

But Michael grabbed her before she could go, pulling her close enough to whisper in her ear. "If there was any other way..."

She heard the regret, the guilt, in his voice. Maybe he wasn't so ruthless after all. She closed her eyes, wishing they had met in another time. Another place.

But wishful thinking wouldn't accomplish anything.

"Fifteen minutes," she whispered, then pulled away from him.

It took her three minutes to race up the stairs to the third floor, then jimmy the lock to Seamus's room. Once inside, she closed the door behind her, flipping the lock. Then she turned on the light. There was simply no time for finding her way in the dark, even if she was familiar with the room.

Michael had told her where the safe was located, so she walked straight to it, pulling back the faux window curtain that concealed it.

Rubbing the pad of her thumb over her fingertips, she leaned as closely as possible to the steel safe, aware that she could feel telltale vibrations from the lock with her body as well as with her hands.

Five more minutes ticked by as she slowly spun the dial. Perspiration beaded her brow when she found the first number.

Two.

Three minutes later she sensed another slight give in the dial.

Fifteen.

Only one more number...

Every shadow and creak in the house made her jumpy. Once, Sarah thought she heard footsteps in the hallway, but finally decided it was just her imagination.

With only a few minutes left to spare, she detected the third number.

Twenty-two.

The safe opened and she quickly rifled through the contents until she found a thick envelope.

"Last Will and Testament of Seamus Q. Wolff."

Sarah breathed a sigh of relief as she pulled it out

of the safe. Then she felt a heavy tap on her shoulder. Almost jumping our of her shoes, she turned to see that the door to the safe had swung against her.

Heart pounding, she pushed the steel safe door fully open again. But a few moments later, it swung back, bouncing against her shoulder.

The combination kept echoing through her head. *Two. Fifteen. Twenty-two.* She hesitated for a moment, wondering why it sounded familiar. Two. Fifteen. Twenty-two.

February 15, 1922.

Her grandmother's birthday. Coincidence? Sarah didn't think so, but she didn't have time to ponder it now.

Realizing that door wouldn't stay open on its own, Sarah had a new puzzle to figure out. Michael wanted the safe standing wide open so the theft of the will would be detected immediately. He believed that would put an end to any more "accidents," at least for a while.

But the safe wouldn't stay open. She knew she had to find something to wedge against the bottom hinge, something that wouldn't look too obvious.

She chose a small envelope, glancing perfunctorily at the front of it. Then she blinked and looked again.

The letter was addressed to Seamus Wolff, postmarked in the year 1942.

And it was from her grandmother.

MICHAEL WORE A PATH across the antique rug in the alcove, feeling like the ruthless son of a bitch so many people accused him of being.

He checked his watch, not sure he could wait any longer. She'd been gone thirteen minutes. Had one of the servants caught her? Had the safe proved too difficult to crack? Had she scooped up some money along with the will and was now making a quick getaway?

No. He knew that wasn't possible. Not only because she'd made it clear she'd do anything to protect her grandfather—just like him—but because Sarah Hewitt wasn't made that way. He knew it down to his soul.

She also wasn't a thief—until now.

Thanks to him.

Michael checked his watch again, deciding he'd waited long enough. It was time to go after her.

But the sound of his grandfather's voice stopped him cold.

"Michael?" Seamus's deep voice echoed in the long gallery.

He took a deep breath, then stepped out of the alcove. "Yes?"

Seamus wheeled his chair around, his brow crinkled. "I realize it's your birthday, but you've been ignoring your guests long enough."

The last thing Michael needed was a lecture on

party etiquette, not when he was so worried about Sarah he could barely think straight.

Then she suddenly stepped out of the alcove and stood beside him. Michael was so relieved to see her that a stupid grin split his face. He turned to her and said, "I'm about to be grounded for ignoring my guests."

"It's my fault, Seamus," she explained, a hot flush on her cheeks. She sounded slightly out of breath. "I told Michael I wanted a private tour."

Seamus looked back and forth between the two of them, his eyebrows arching toward the ceiling. He obviously had the wrong idea about what they'd been doing in the alcove. "Well, like I said before, it is his birthday."

Michael circled his arm around Sarah's waist, so glad she was back safely that he still couldn't think straight. He pulled her close to him, enjoying the friction of her body against him. Wishing their clothes weren't in the way.

"You two go ahead and enjoy yourselves," Seamus said, slowly spinning his wheelchair around. "I can handle the guests."

When they were alone again, Michael turned to her, tenderly brushing a stray curl off her cheek. "Are you all right?"

She shrugged away his concern. "I'm fine."

He couldn't seem to stop touching her. His hands at her waist, then cupping her face. "You're sure?"

"Positive," she assured him. "I left the door to the safe open, just like you instructed. The will is..."

"Not now," he interjected over a wild whoop of laughter at the far end of the gallery. "Maureen's about at her limit of cosmopolitans, so the party should be breaking up soon. You can give me the will later."

"When?" she asked, the sparkle of the diamonds at her slender throat reflecting in her green eyes.

He could see impatience there, too. Was she that anxious to get away from him now that she'd fulfilled her end of their agreement?

Michael leaned toward her and whispered, "Meet me at midnight."

10

LATER THAT NIGHT, Sarah kicked off her heels in her bedroom, relishing the feel of her bare feet sinking into the carpet. Then she picked up the fifty-year-old letter she'd left under her pillow. A letter to Seamus Wolff from her grandmother. A letter he'd kept all this time.

She knew reading it was an invasion of privacy, but her curiosity got the better of her. Maybe this letter would help explain the five-decade feud between the Hewitts and the Wolffs. Maybe it would reveal the reason why Seamus and Bertram had carried their animosity for each other so long.

Opening the envelope, she pulled out the thin pink stationery and unfolded the letter. Her throat tightened at the sight of her grandmother's familiar, graceful handwriting.

Dear Seamus,
What happened between us last night was a mistake. I love Bertram. I know that's not what you want to hear, but I must follow my heart. You're a good man, Seamus. You deserve a

good woman. I'm not that woman, but my sincere hope is that someday you find her.

All I ask is that you keep what happened between us to yourself. Revealing it will not change anything and I fear you will be the only one who is hurt in the end.

I know how much Bertram values your friendship. The last thing I want to do is come between the two of you. In time, you will realize that I am right. Until then, I ask that you not contact me again.

Anna

Sarah read the letter again, her heart in her throat. Seamus and her grandmother? A love triangle? An illicit tryst?

The last memory she had of her beloved grandmother was as a frail and white-haired old woman, sick and confined to her bed, insisting no one make any fuss over her.

But there was no doubt she'd once been a lovely, vivacious young woman. Sarah had seen it in the family photo album, including pictures from Anna and Bertram's wedding.

Sarah remembered how the joy had radiated from her face. How her love for her handsome young husband had been so evident in her smiling eyes.

What happened between us last night was a mistake.

Was it possible? Sarah wasn't naive enough to think her generation had invented sex. Hormones raged just as strongly in 1942 as they did now. She knew from all too recent experience how easy it was to make a mistake, to succumb to the passion of the moment.

Did her grandfather know? Was that the reason his hatred for Seamus Wolff ran so deep? If so, he'd never shown anything but the greatest love and kindness to her grandmother. She could be grateful for that at least.

I must follow my heart.

That's what Sarah had been trying so desperately *not* to do. As much as she hated to admit it, her heart wanted Michael. Or rather, the man who had made such passionate love to her on New Year's Eve. Not the man who'd coerced her into committing a crime.

But he did it for his grandfather.

Sarah mentally shook herself, wanting to silence that voice that came straight from her heart. Even now she was making excuses for him.

This was why she couldn't risk listening to her own treacherous heart. It was too eager to believe that Michael's interest in her was more than purely physical, more than a fleeting attraction.

Although, she couldn't deny the sexual pull between them. Not when she battled it every time she saw him, and every night in her dreams.

That's why she had to leave this house as soon as possible, before her heart and her hormones overruled her common sense.

The mantel clock in her room struck midnight, its muted gong reverberating through her. After carefully folding the letter, she returned it to the envelope, then placed it in her picnic basket.

Sarah walked over to her bed and pulled up one corner of the mattress, dipping her hand deep inside the fitted sheet. After searching for a moment, she pulled out the large envelope, smoothing her hand over the front cover.

She sincerely hoped Michael hadn't made a big mistake. Then she took a deep, fortifying breath and headed for the door.

The hallway was clear, no sound coming from any of the bedrooms. Sarah stepped out onto the marble tile, ice-cold on her bare feet. She walked to Michael's room, then tapped softly on the door.

When no one answered, she turned the knob and pushed the door open. Then she walked inside the room, closing the door quickly behind her.

At first, she thought the room was empty. Only a small lamp burned, casting long shadows over the bed. Then she saw him standing by the window, a crystal tumbler in his hand.

She moved deeper inside the room. "I brought you Seamus's will."

He didn't reply or even turn around, just kept staring out at the moonlit mountainside.

Sarah moved beside him, the will in her outstretched hand. But Michael just tipped up his glass, the ice clinking as he drained it.

He still wore his tuxedo, though the black tie hung loose around his neck and the top two buttons of his crisp white shirt were undone.

His dark hair was rumpled, as if he'd been running his hands through it. She sensed a certain wildness in him tonight. Something that couldn't quite be explained by too much to drink.

"I'll be gone in the morning," she said softly, as she set the envelope on the windowsill. Then she turned around to leave.

"What about the necklace?"

Sarah paused, lifting one hand to her throat. She'd almost forgotten about it. "I'll leave it in my room, along with the dress and the shoes and...everything."

He turned to face her, something undefinable glittering in his gray eyes. "That clasp is tricky. You'll need help with it."

"I can call Maria," she said, her heart skittering as he slowly walked toward her.

"Maria's asleep." He stood behind her now, his hands lightly on her shoulders. "Let me."

Sarah knew she'd sound like either a coward or a

fool to refuse him. Giving a slight nod, she lifted the wisps of her hair off the back of her neck to give him better access to the clasp.

"So perfect," he breathed, his hands sliding gently over her bare shoulders.

Heat pooled low inside her at his touch and she closed her eyes. "Michael, please, I..."

"Let me," he whispered huskily, then tenderly kissed the nape of her neck. His lips moved over the curve of her shoulder as his hands glided down her arms and circled her waist.

Sarah stood unmoving in his loose embrace, her back against his broad chest. She was afraid to move. Afraid not to move. The sensation of his hands and mouth on her body made rational thinking impossible.

When his hands slid up over her rib cage to cup her breasts, she tipped her head back onto his broad shoulder with a soft moan.

"So sweet," Michael breathed, his mouth at her throat now. His fingers swirled over the tips of her breasts until her nipples strained against the gossamer fabric.

He turned her in his arms and pulled her flush against his hard, hot body.

"So...mine," he growled, before capturing her mouth with his own.

Sarah was utterly lost then. His desire engulfed

her. She heard it in his voice, saw it in his eyes, felt it in his kiss.

She circled her arms around his neck to hang on as he deepened the kiss, his hands pulling her hips flush against his full arousal. She wanted to be even closer. To touch that place deep inside of him where he never let anyone go. To know the real Michael Wolff.

Parting her lips, she tasted the brandy on his tongue as it stroked inside her mouth, intoxicating her with his passion. He groaned low when she kissed him back, meeting his heat with her own.

The elixir of desire spiraled through her blood, making her wild and wanton. She pulled her gown up far enough to swing one leg around his waist. She rocked against him as he kissed her over and over again.

Michael groaned aloud, pressing her hips against him. But when he scooped her up into his arms and carried her to his bed, the first twinge of apprehension sobered her, allowing those pesky doubts to seep into her mind.

Making love to Michael would result in serious consequences. For her, anyway. She'd likely lose her pride. Most definitely lose her heart.

But what about him? Did he just want to acquire her, like a piece of Egyptian art? Something he could look at and display until he had no use for it anymore?

Then he kissed her again, holding her in his lap on the edge of the bed. His hand slipped one thin strap of her gown off of her shoulder, until her breast spilled out of the bodice.

Sarah wanted to stop him, but when he bent his head and took her breast in his mouth, she found herself tangling her fingers in his hair instead, pulling him closer as his tongue swirled around her nipple.

The next thing she knew, they were both lying on the bed and Michael's hands had found the zipper at the back of her dress.

The sound of it slowly sliding down turned her passion into panic. She pulled away from him, trying to catch her breath. "I have to go."

"Not yet," he said, reaching for her.

But she rose off the bed, her gown hanging halfway off of her. She clutched it to her chest, her body still thrumming.

He rose to his feet, confusion etched on his face. "What's wrong?"

"I didn't want this to happen again," she sputtered, grappling to pull up the loose ends of her gown. "I'm leaving now. For good."

He set his jaw. "No, you're not."

She blinked up at him. "But we had a deal. If I

broke into Seamus's safe and stole his will, you promised you'd let me go."

"That was only part of it," he said, his eyes smoldering as he took a step closer to her. "You also agreed to act as my grandfather's caretaker. He's not fully recovered yet."

She stared up at him, suddenly understanding how he got his ruthless reputation. "You're not planning to let me go until I sleep with you," she stated bluntly.

"You want me," Michael replied, not bothering to deny it. "I know you do."

"This won't work," she said, as the heat he'd generated inside of her turned into molten anger. "You can't blackmail someone into loving you!"

"I never asked you to love me," Michael bit out. "I'm not that stupid. I just want you in my bed. And judging from your reaction a few minutes ago, you want the same thing. So why do we have to make this complicated?"

Sarah knew she'd probably be wasting her breath telling him the reason, but decided to try anyway. "I'm not just a walking vat of hormones, Michael. I want a man who desires my heart and my mind as much as my body."

"Or maybe you're just afraid," he challenged. "That's why you're in such a hurry to run away. Because if you stay, you know you won't be able to resist this thing between us anymore."

"You're right," she admitted, lifting her chin. "And if we make love while you're keeping me prisoner in this house, that makes me nothing more than your sex slave."

He pulled her into his arms with a growl of pure frustration. "I'm the one who's a prisoner. I can't stop thinking about you. I can't stop wanting you every minute of every day."

She gripped his shoulders to keep him from pulling her closer, and to keep herself from falling into his arms once more.

"We're too different." She thought about the dinner party tonight, how alien she'd felt from the rest of his guests. "We're from two different worlds."

"Then come into my world," he implored. "I'll buy you a townhouse. I'll give you anything you want."

His offer made her twist away from him. "So I can go from sex slave to mistress? No thanks."

"That's not what I meant." He raked his fingers through his hair. "Hell, I don't know what I meant. We'll talk about it in the morning."

"No." She moved toward the door. "We won't."

"Sarah..."

She walked out of his room without a backward glance. Pain and anger and confusion were whirling inside of her. As she closed the door behind her, she looked up to see Blair walking toward her in the hallway. Sarah realized the disshelved state of her gown and her hair left little mystery as to what she'd been doing in Michael's room.

Blair looked from Sarah's to Michael's door and back again, her thin blond brow raised in speculation. "Wishing Michael a happy birthday?"

"Yes," Sarah said hastily, brushing past her. "Good night."

Blair turned to stare after her. "Good night."

Sarah slammed into her room and retrieved her suitcases from the closet, tossing them onto the bed.

She'd thrown in half her clothes before she realized she couldn't leave, not when there was the slightest chance that Michael might carry through on his threat to turn that security tape over to the police.

But he couldn't keep her prisoner here forever. Could he?

11

THE NEXT MORNING, Michael awoke with a pounding, brandy-induced headache, the sound of his grandfather's enraged roar in his ears.

Stumbling out of bed, he pulled on his robe, cinching it at the waist as he moved toward the door.

Images from last night tumbled through his mind. Sarah looking like a princess in her white gown. The way she'd lifted her hair off her neck when he'd unclasped the diamond necklace. The shock in her eyes when he'd all but asked her to be his mistress.

Hell. He hadn't intended it that way, but in the sober light of day, he saw that no one could take his proposition any other way.

Michael walked across the hallway to his grandfather's suite, the door already ajar. Sarah stood inside, also in her robe. She glanced at Michael and then away again, a blush now staining her cheeks.

He wanted to explain last night, to blame his loutish behavior on too much brandy. But the truth was that he'd simply been drunk with desire for her. Michael knew he owed her an apology, but one look at his grandfather's livid face told him now was not the time for it.

"What's wrong?" he asked Seamus, who leaned on his walker near the open safe. Blair stood beside him in a black silk robe, looking as if she wanted nothing more than to go back to sleep.

"Call the police," Seamus demanded. "Somebody broke in here last night and rifled through my safe."

Michael thought he'd been prepared for his grandfather's reaction. But the reality of it hit him like a sucker punch in the gut. The indignation reverberating from his grandfather made him wonder once again if he'd really had the right to take such a drastic step. Guilt pounded against his temple and he wished he'd popped some aspirin before dealing with this situation. Time for damage control.

"Is anything missing?" Michael asked, knowing he had to play dumb and hating every minute of it. He didn't look at Sarah, afraid of what he might see in her eyes.

Seamus's hands clenched the arms of his walker. "Hell, yes, something is missing. A letter—a *private* letter—addressed to me."

This wasn't in the script. Michael looked at the open safe, knowing she'd brought him the envelope containing the will. Only Michael hadn't taken the time to look inside the envelope. He'd been too focused on Sarah.

Had she made a mistake? Or worse, tried to deceive him again? Michael rubbed one hand over his jaw, the events of the night before still a little fuzzy. He remembered how anxious she'd been to leave last night. The anger flashing in her green eyes when he'd threatened her with the security tape again. She'd fooled him once before. Why should he doubt that she'd try to do it again?

But Michael didn't want to believe it. Even as Blair began to take inventory of the rest of the contents of the safe, he kept telling himself there had to be some kind of mistake.

Seamus pounded his walker on the floor to get Michael's attention. "Well, what are you waiting for? Call the police. I want to file charges."

Michael knew he had to play this very carefully. Despite all their precautions, he couldn't take the chance that the police might find evidence of Sarah's involvement. "Let's make an inventory first. If the only thing missing is a letter..."

"The will!" Blair whirled around, her eyes wide and furious. "The will is gone."

"Are you sure?" Michael asked, relieved and confused at the same time. So Sarah had taken the will after all. But what about this mysterious letter? And why was it so important to his grandfather?

"Of course I'm sure." Blair's gaze bounced between Michael and Sarah. "And I think I know who took it."

He sensed Sarah tensing beside him and resisted the urge to put his arm around her. He'd learned last night she didn't need or want anyone to protect her—especially him.

"I think we'd better be careful not to start flinging accusations around," Michael admonished, "especially when we don't have any proof."

"We don't need proof," Blair countered. "You're the only one with a motive."

Then she turned to her husband, knowing he was the one she had to convince. "Michael has never liked me or approved of our marriage. I'm sure he wasn't happy when you wrote that new will, leaving everything to me and him out in the cold."

"That's bunk," Seamus said with a snort. "My grandson is already almost as rich as me. He doesn't need or want my money."

"I wouldn't be so sure," Blair retorted. "All he seems to care about is money. Plotting all those hostile takeovers and corporate buyouts. I think he cares more about money than people."

Before Michael could accuse Blair of the same, Sarah stepped in to defend him. "That's not fair."

All three of them turned to look at her. Michael couldn't believe she was trying to protect him, especially after the way he'd treated her last night.

Too late she seemed to realize how defensive she sounded. Sarah licked her lips, considering her words more carefully now. "I just think it's important not to overreact in this kind of situation."

"And I think you and Michael are in on this together," Blair accused. "After all, I caught you coming out of his bedroom last night."

He closed his eyes, wondering if this day could possibly get any worse. It didn't take him long to find out.

Blair turned to her husband again, placing one hand on his forearm. "I know this is hard for you, Seamus. But it's the only explanation."

"You're wrong about that." Seamus shook her off. "I already know who did it. Bertram Hewitt."

Sarah blanched. "What?"

"The man is a nutcase," Seamus explained, taking her shock for confusion. "He's had some crazy vendetta against me for too many years to count. And Bertram's broken into this house before," he looked up at Sarah, "to steal that very diamond necklace you wore last night."

Sarah opened her mouth, but no words came out, her eyes wide with horror.

Michael knew he had to intervene before all hell broke loose. The only reason Sarah had agreed to move in here and steal the will was to protect her felonious grandfather. Only now Bertram was being accused of a crime he didn't commit.

"Let's think about this for a minute," Michael began, trying to stay calm. "It's been years since Hewitt went to prison for stealing that necklace. Why would he want it again now?"

"Because Bertram contacted me a couple of months ago," Seamus announced. "Said that we both know I cheated him and that it was time I made everything right. That he deserved his fair share. That his family shouldn't have to suffer anymore."

Michael saw Sarah pale. He wanted to reach out and hold her, to assure her everything would be all right. Only, he couldn't be sure himself. He'd never seen his grandfather this furious before.

"What about the tape?" Blair said, looking toward the safe. "The security camera probably recorded everything. All we have to do is watch it to catch the culprit."

Michael walked over to the safe, then slid the panel on the adjacent wall to reveal the camera. He popped the tape out and held it up. "Here it is."

What Blair and Seamus didn't know was that he'd disengaged the security system last evening, so the camera hadn't been running at all when Sarah broke into the safe.

"There's our proof that Bertram Hewitt is behind this," Seamus said with conviction. "Probably learned all kinds of dirty tricks while he was in prison. Thinks he's too smart to get caught this time."

Blair pressed her lips firmly together, her cheeks flushed with anger.

"Bertram stole my letter and my will." His jaw clenched. "I know it."

"None of us know anything yet," Michael countered. "So before we start flinging wild accusations at the police, let me contact Cole Rafferty. He can investigate this for us without involving the police."

Now he just hoped he could pull Cole away from his newborn daughter.

"How convenient for you," Blair said wryly. "That the investigator you want to hire also happens to be your best friend."

Michael knew he could never reason with her, so he turned to Seamus. "If we involve the police, they'll suspect everyone who was at the party last night—people we do business with who definitely won't appreciate being the focus of a criminal investigation."

Seamus hesitated, then gave a stiff nod. "You're right. Contact your investigator so we can keep this matter under our control. When we have something solid against Hewitt, we'll go to the police."

Michael breathed a silent sigh of relief. "I'll take care of everything."

"But what about the will?" Blair cried. "An investigation could take forever. I think you should write a new will. Right now."

Seamus scowled. "While I'm still in my pajamas?"

"Michael and Sarah can be the witnesses," Blair said, undeterred. She gave them both a tight smile. "I'm sure they won't mind if they truly are innocent."

Silence grew heavy in the room as Seamus turned to look at his wife. "Why the big hurry? It's almost as if you expect me to keel over at any moment."

"No, of course not," she exclaimed, backpedaling now. "The doctor said you're in the best of health for a man..."

"Of my age," Seamus finished for her. "Seems like that damn will is more important to you than I am."

Blair paled. "That's not true, Seamus. You know that. I just think it's odd that someone would steal your will. I mean, it's obviously an attack on me, since I'm the main beneficiary."

He shook his head. "Hewitt's behind this. Probably thinks he can tie up my estate if I kick off before he gets his hands on that necklace. Just goes to show he's not as clever as he thinks."

Blair knelt down beside his walker, placing her slender hand over his wrinkled one. "Then let's prove him wrong. Let's put together a new will."

"All right," Seamus conceded. "We'll do it."

A smile lit her face. "Good."

"As soon as my lawyer gets back into town," Seamus added.

Her smile faded. "But that won't be for at least another month."

He arched a grizzled brow. "So?"

She hesitated, then swallowed. "That sounds fine, Seamus. Whatever makes you happy, makes me happy."

"Good. Now I want to go back to bed. I've been standing on this bum hip for too long already."

Blair rose to her feet. "I'll help you."

"No," he replied, shifting away from her. "I want Sarah to help me."

Watching Blair's expression, Michael almost felt sorry for the woman—if she hadn't revealed herself so completely just now. At least Seamus was finally able to see her true colors.

Now was the time to bring to light any evidence his investigator had found against her.

Michael moved toward the door, glancing back to see Sarah helping Seamus onto the bed. She treated his grandfather with such gentleness. So in contrast to the hellcat she'd been with him last night.

Sweet and innocent. Wild and wanton. At one time, he'd wondered which was the real Sarah. Now he knew the answer was both.

It just made him want her more than ever.

AN HOUR LATER, Sarah walked out of Seamus's room, closing the door softly behind her so she wouldn't wake him.

Michael was waiting for her in the hallway. He was dressed in a suit and tie now, his hair combed and his square jaw clean-shaven. Maureen had been right. The man was lethal.

"How is he?" Michael asked in a near whisper.

"Exhausted," she replied, stepping closer so he could hear her, "and quite upset. I've never seen Seamus so agitated, even when I took his whiskey away."

He glanced at the closed door. "Is Blair with him?"

"She left about thirty minutes ago. Seamus wouldn't look at her."

Michael's nostrils flared. "You blame me for that?"

"Who else is responsible for all this mess?" Sarah retorted, her own nerves still raw. After everything she'd done to protect her grandfather, he'd already been named as the prime suspect in the theft. "You're the one who made me steal that will."

"But I didn't tell you to take some letter, too. What's that about?"

"It's a long story." Sarah massaged her temple with her fingertips, a headache starting to throb. She'd lain awake long into the night, too upset about her midnight rendezvous to sleep, too nervous about the morning to come.

"I'm not going anywhere until you tell me."

He didn't leave her much choice. She moved toward her bedroom. "I think it will be easier if I show you."

Sarah could feel Michael's gaze on her as she walked through the door and toward the dresser. She'd hid the letter inside a box of Napoleon's dog biscuits. A little extreme perhaps, but she didn't know for certain if Seamus would demand a search of the house from top to bottom when he found out someone had broken into his safe.

When she handed Michael the pink envelope, he grimaced as he brushed the dog biscuit crumbs off of it. Then he pulled out the letter, his gaze quickly scanning the page. "Who's Anna?"

"My grandmother."

He looked up at her. "They had an affair?"

"We don't know that," Sarah replied, taking the letter out of his hands and placing it back in the envelope.

"It sounds pretty clear to me."

He moved closer to her and her senses went on high alert. What if he kissed her again? Her lips actually tingled at the thought.

"So is this how the silly feud between them got started?" he asked. "Over a woman?"

"I don't know," she answered honestly. "According to my grandfather, it's all about the necklace."

Michael looked thoughtful. "You saw how my grandfather reacted when he realized that letter was missing. I'd say it was about a lot more than the necklace."

"I guess we'll never know for certain."

"At least it proved the Wolff jinx is alive and well."

"What jinx?"

Michael arched a brow. "Haven't you heard? Money can't buy love."

She studied him for a long moment. "So you believe your fortune excludes you from ever finding your true love?"

"My grandfather's superstitious," he said, hedging her question. "It's those Irish roots."

She sensed Seamus wasn't the only one who believed it. And why wouldn't Michael be skeptical? He'd seen his grandfather's five marriages fall apart, with the sixth one now teetering on the brink. His own parents had split up for some reason she still hadn't learned.

Was that why he was still single? Because he believed he was jinxed?

"Plenty of marriages fail," she said, "although often it's because there's a lack of money, not too much."

"Your grandparents stayed together. Anna chose Bertram over my grandfather and obviously didn't regret it. I think we both know he would have taken her back at any time. That he still loves her to this day."

She turned the pink envelope over in her hands, remembering the anguish she'd seen in Seamus's eyes this morning. "I never should have taken his letter. But when I saw my grandmother's name on the envelope, my curiosity got the better of me."

Sarah looked up into Michael's eyes. "I honestly didn't think he would miss it. And now I don't know how to give it back to him without raising even more suspicion."

Michael reached out to take the envelope, his fingers lingering on her hand. "Don't worry. I'll have Cole return it to him in a couple of days. He can say he found it lying on the drive."

"So you really do plan to hire an investigator?"

"I already have," he replied. "But not for the theft of the will, naturally. I'm trying to gather evidence against Blair. After what happened this morning, I don't think it will be too hard to convince Seamus that she's behind those accidents."

"And when you do?" she asked, wondering if he'd even considered the ripple effect of his actions.

"Then he can get rid of her."

She stared up at him. "You make it sound so easy, so...cold."

Michael met her gaze. "You think I like this? Hell, I've watched my grandfather marry one woman after the other, waiting for one of them to love him. But it's always about the money. Every single time."

She could hear more than anger in his voice. There was pain, too. "Why do I get the feeling we're not just talking about your grandfather anymore?"

"Because you think too much." He turned toward the door, his broad back as rigid as a brick wall. "I have to go to work. Watch out for him, okay?"

"I will," she promised, wondering how to knock that wall down. But maybe she wouldn't like what she found on the other side.

He turned at the door. "About last night. I want to apologize. I promise it won't happen again."

Then he was gone.

Sarah stared after him, thinking of everything that had gone on between them last night. The kiss. The proposition. The passion.

What exactly had Michael Wolff just promised never to do again?

12

"ONLY A FEW MORE STEPS," Sarah said, as she walked along the hallway with Seamus. She held his arm, but he barely leaned on her, preferring to transfer his weight to his brand-new cane.

"It's hell to be old," he muttered, his breath coming in deep gasps.

Seamus had been pushing his physical therapy in the week since the safe incident, demanding Sarah help him learn to walk again or he'd do it himself. He was actually making tremendous progress, though she could see the pain now etched on his perspiring face.

They reached his room at last and Sarah helped him into a chair. He collapsed against it, his cane falling to the floor.

Sarah picked it up and leaned it against his chair. "I told you we shouldn't have made that second trip down the hall."

"That's because you're a nag." He leaned his head back, but she could still see the spark of mischief glittering in his brown eyes. "Or maybe just afraid I'd leave you in the dust."

She smiled, glad to see his mood improve along with his health. The man had a wicked sense of humor and a sharp wit. Much like his grandson.

Not that she'd seen much of either in Michael lately, simply because she hadn't seen him. He'd maintained his distance, keeping the promise he'd made to her. No more lingering glances. No more accidental touches. No more hot kisses in the hallway.

Sarah tried to tell herself it didn't matter. That nothing could come of her feelings for Michael, a man who believed he was jinxed by love!

As she poured Seamus a glass of water from the pitcher, her gaze fell on her grandmother's letter. Cole Rafferty had returned it to him a few days ago, just as Michael had promised.

Seamus had kept the letter on the nightstand next to his bed ever since.

"Don't tell me you're a snoop as well as a nag," Seamus teased, following her gaze.

She smiled, then handed him the glass. "I'll admit I'd like to know why that old letter is so important to you."

"So would my wife." Seamus took a long sip from the glass, then smacked his lips and emitted a deep, satisfied sigh. "But it's nothing more than a Dear John letter. Can you believe a woman actually turned down a handsome coot like me?"

His smile didn't quite reach his eyes. Sarah leaned

against a chair. "The lady must have had a good reason."

He shrugged. "Not good enough for me."

"You loved her very much." It was a statement, not a question.

For a while, she didn't think he was going to answer her. Then he stared into his glass. "Sad to say, Anna was the only woman I've ever really loved. The only one I've ever known who truly cared about me."

Her throat tightened at the tone of his voice. "Blair cares about you."

"Blair needs me." Seamus took another sip from his glass. "There's a big difference. Now get out of here. I'm tired."

So much for his good mood. But Sarah knew it was her own fault for bringing up a sore subject, even fifty years later.

After she tucked him into his bed for a nap, Sarah went down to the sunroom on the first floor to play with her dog. Napoleon was thrilled to see her and looked fatter than ever.

She tossed a rubber ball in her hand. "Spoiled rotten, I see."

Napoleon jumped around her ankles, almost beside himself with joy. When she tossed the ball, he gave a yelp and scurried after it.

But even Nappy couldn't make her forget the conversation she'd just had with Seamus. The sadness in his eyes. The note of regret in his voice.

She'd been telling herself that leaving this house and Michael behind would be the best way to forget the passion he'd brought to her life, the way he'd touched her soul the way no man ever had before. But what if Sarah couldn't forget him? What if fifty years from now, she was the one wishing for what might have been?

When Napoleon scampered back with the ball clamped between his teeth, she scooped him up and held him close to her.

"What should I do, Nappy?"

The cairn terrier barked his reply, causing the ball to fall out of his mouth and bounce onto the floor. He scampered out of her arms to chase it again.

There were no answers for her here. She had to look into her heart.

Later that afternoon, after spending useless hours avoiding what had been on her mind, she tapped lightly on Seamus's door, then walked inside. He lay in a deep sleep on his bed, the water pitcher half-empty beside him, his face slack.

Reaching into the drawer of his nightstand, she pulled out his pain medication. As she leaned over to pat his shoulder, Sarah inwardly chastised herself for letting him indulge in such a strenuous workout today. "Wake up, Seamus. Time for your pill."

She hated to rouse him, but she knew if he didn't take his medication on schedule it wasn't as effective. "Seamus?"

He didn't move.

She shook him harder now, raising her voice. "Seamus! Wake up."

Still no response.

Apprehension skittered up Sarah's spine when his head lolled to one side, his skin tone slightly gray. She pried one of his eyelids open and saw the eyeball rolled back in his head.

Something was very wrong.

MICHAEL SAW the ambulance as soon as he drove through the front gate. He parked beside it, catapulting out of his car and running for the front door. He was gasping for breath by the time he reached the third floor, his chest aching.

Sarah stood outside his grandfather's door, turning when she heard him running down the hallway. The expression on her face turned his blood to ice.

"What happened?" he cried.

She reached out to stop him from bursting into his grandfather's room. "I found Seamus unconscious in his bed. The paramedics are with him now. So is his doctor. Blair called him."

That explained the other car in the driveway. But

why hadn't the ambulance taken him to the hospital? Was he too critical to move?

"What's the matter with him?"

She grasped his hands in her own, her touch calming him. "I heard the paramedics say something about a possible poisoning. Then they kicked me out of the room. We're supposed to wait for the doctor's report."

Poison? He stumbled back a step, aware that he'd failed to protect his grandfather. Seamus had stepped into the place of his parents, loving him unconditionally, never letting him down. Michael wished he could say the same.

"Blair's in with your grandfather now," Sarah told him, then seeing the expression on his face, gave his hands a reassuring squeeze. "Don't worry. Nothing can happen to him with the doctor and paramedics in there, too."

"Unless it's too late." He wrapped his arms tightly around Sarah, breaking the promise he'd made to her a week ago. Right now he needed to hold on to something sweet and good, to warm the cold emptiness that now threatened to overwhelm him.

Sarah let him hold her, anchoring him from the chaos swirling around his heart. Her presence calmed him and he pondered how that was possible since most of the time she left his senses reeling.

"I thought getting rid of that will would solve the

problem," he whispered against her hair. "I thought she'd give up."

"We don't know Blair is to blame," Sarah said softly. Then she reached up to cup his cheeks in her hands. "You look awful. Why don't you sit down and try to relax?"

Michael wanted to keep holding her. Instead, he followed her advice, seating himself on a small ornamental bench in the hallway.

He stared at Seamus's door as Sarah sat down beside him. What the hell was taking so long?

"Blair looked worried, too," Sarah told him.

Michael turned to her. "Cole turned in his background report on her today."

"And?"

"And Blair isn't her real name. Neither was Ballingham."

She sighed. "There's something incredibly sad about investigating a member of your own family."

"In this case, it's necessary," he replied. "Her real name is Casey Winters. She grew up dirt-poor in a small town in Oklahoma. Married when she was twenty. Has three kids. They live with her sister. Guess who's sending them money every month?"

"That doesn't necessarily make her a bad person. Or a potential murderer."

"But it does make her a liar." His gut clenched. "My grandfather doesn't know any of this. She fed him some cockamamie story about attending the best boarding schools in Europe, then dropping out of Vassar to become a model."

"If anything happens to Grandfather..." His voice broke and he sucked in a deep breath. "He's the only family I have left, the one person in the world who cares about me."

She reached for his hand. "That's not true."

He met her gaze and his heart flipped over in his chest. But before he could ask her to elaborate, the bedroom door opened and the doctor walked out.

Michael rose to his feet, Sarah beside him. "Well?"

"Seamus Wolff is the toughest seventy-year-old man I've ever met," Dr. Kluver said. "He should make a complete recovery."

Michael could finally breathe again. "Thank you, doctor."

"You're quite welcome."

Sarah cleared her throat. "The paramedics mentioned something about poison...."

"In a matter of speaking," Dr. Kluver replied. "Seamus accidentally ingested too much alcohol for his current level of pain medication. That can be a deadly combination."

Sarah shook her head. "That's not possible. I removed all the alcohol from his room."

The doctor removed his glasses, rubbing the

lenses on the edge of his suitcoat. "Not quite. The water pitcher on his nightstand is half-full of gin."

"Gin?" Her jaw dropped and her green eyes filled with remorse.

"Don't," Michael admonished, before she could start blaming herself. "My grandfather has always been stubborn. If he wanted to drink, there was nothing you could have done to stop him."

"You don't understand. It *is* my fault. I made him bring up the past. The letter."

"I'm not sure if this will make you feel better or worse," the doctor told her. "But Seamus admitted that he's been spiking his water pitcher with gin for the past week. Only it seems this time he drank just enough to cause a reaction."

"I guess I make a lousy caretaker." She looked up at Michael. "Looks like you picked the wrong girl for the job."

But the right girl for his bed. His heart. He just wished he could find a way to convince her of that.

The doctor cleared his throat. "I should be on my way now. Please give me a call if there are any further developments. And hide all the gin."

"We will." Michael extended his hand. "Thank you, Dr. Kluver. I appreciate you coming all the way out here."

Shaking Michael's hand, the doctor chuckled. "I don't think Seamus feels the same. As soon as he regained consciousness, he told me to get my fat ass back to the city. Thinks I'm going to charge him a fortune for the house call, which I am."

The doctor was still chuckling as he turned and walked away. Michael waited until he disappeared around the corner before he turned back to Sarah.

"I absolutely forbid you to feel guilty about what happened."

That brought a half smile to her lips. "You can't control everything, Michael, no matter how hard you try."

She didn't need to remind him. If he could control everything, his mother would still be in his life. His father wouldn't have died in a plane crash. Sarah wouldn't want to leave him.

"I'm fine," Sarah assured him. "Really." Then she gave him a gentle shove toward Seamus's room. "Now go in and see your grandfather. That will make you both feel better."

Michael walked into the bedroom, realizing too late that Sarah hadn't followed him. He turned around to see the empty doorway and felt the same emptiness in his heart.

Seamus watched him from the bed, his eyelids beginning to droop. But he did manage to spit out three words before drifting off to sleep.

"Love is hell."

MICHAEL EXITED Seamus's room as the hall clock struck eleven times. His grandfather had slept most of the evening and Michael had watched him, assuring himself he was all right.

Blair had kept a vigil on the opposite side of Seamus's bed, finally retiring to a separate room, claiming she didn't want to disturb her husband.

So everyone in the Wolff house was sleeping alone tonight. He slowed his pace as he walked past Sarah's door, remembering their earlier conversation.

He's the only one in the world who cares about me. Who loves me.

That's not true.

Michael stopped walking, his pulse pounding in his ears. What had she meant? If the doctor hadn't emerged from his grandfather's room at that moment, he would have asked—no, *demanded*—an answer.

Was it possible that Sarah Hewitt cared about him? Even loved him?

He stared at her door, realizing he could never see into her heart, never truly know if she loved him. But at the moment, he didn't care. He just didn't want to be alone anymore.

Michael reached up and tapped his knuckles against her door. His palms grew damp as he waited, like a boy ready to ask a girl on a first date.

He glanced down at his clothes, grimacing at the wrinkles. Hastily straightening his tie, he tried to come up with something clever to say to her when she opened the door. Something to make her smile.

But he never got the chance, because the door never opened.

He raised his hand to knock again, then pulled back. Either she was asleep or she didn't want to see him. If it was the former, he didn't want to wake her. If it was the latter...

Then he had no choice but to turn around and walk away. Because Michael Wolff didn't beg. Not for any woman.

to the police post, made little sense, and spoke harshly enough to keep her warm for the past several nights ahead.

"Because it wasn't true, either," Sarah said.

"And if I promise to behave? The—" He froze, watched

13

ONE WEEK LATER, Sarah walked into Seamus's bedroom suite. "I came to tell you goodbye."

He stood near the window, leaning heavily on his cane. "Leaving me already?"

She smiled. "You fired me, remember?"

In truth, he hadn't needed her help for several days. He was able to walk quite well with his cane, even up and down the stairs. He rarely spent any time in bed anymore. He'd even thrown out his pain medication after the near-catastrophe with the gin.

Seamus turned to look at her. "I don't think my grandson wants you to go."

Sarah steeled herself against the tide of longing that threatened to overwhelm her. She'd practically laid her heart at his feet the other night, but Michael acted as if it had never happened. It was time for her to face the truth. Michael Wolff didn't want her anymore. She needed to move on, before she made a complete fool of herself over him.

At least the fact that she now trusted him enough to keep his word and not turn that security tape over to the police gave her a little comfort, though hardly enough to keep her warm on the cold winter nights ahead.

"I'm sure he won't miss me too much," Sarah said with a cheerfulness she was far from feeling.

"Bull," Seamus exclaimed. "He's in love with you."

Heat flooded her cheeks. "Did he tell you that?"

"Trust me, I know. All a person has to do is see the way he looks at you." Seamus grabbed his cane and limped over to a chair, settling heavily into it.

Sarah didn't know how to respond. Michael hadn't given her any sign that he loved her, or even that he might miss her after she'd gone.

If she wanted proof of that fact, all she had to do was take a look around. The man was nowhere in sight. He knew she was leaving tonight and hadn't even bothered to tell her goodbye.

"He's stubborn," Seamus continued, reading the doubt on her face, "and proud. It runs in the family."

Sarah understood, but she had her pride, too. She'd already revealed her feelings for him. What more could she do?

Kneeling down by the chair, she leaned over to kiss Seamus's grizzled cheek. "Goodbye, Nappy."

"I hate goodbyes," he said hoarsely, not meeting her gaze. "Just go."

Sarah slowly rose to her feet, her heart twisting inside of her. But there was nothing left to say. Besides, Seamus wouldn't want her to stay if he knew she was a Hewitt. And he definitely wouldn't want her for his grandson.

She walked out of his bedroom, then headed toward her own. Her bags were packed and had already been taken down to her car. All she had to do was go to her room and grab her purse and her dog. Then she could go home.

Home. Sarah wasn't sure where that was anymore.

The first thing she noticed when she entered her bedroom was that Napoleon lay sound asleep in the middle of her bed, lightly snoring.

The next thing she noticed was the videotape case. She walked over to the dresser and picked it up. Inside was the 8mm security tape. Michael had kept his promise.

Turning to the television set, she sifted through the collection of standard cassette tapes on the shelf next to it until she found an adapter that would allow her to watch the 8mm tape in the VCR.

Popping the tape in, she hit the fast-forward button, watching silent screen images flashing by. She wanted to erase all evidence of her grandfather's guilt as soon as possible.

Then her stomach dropped to her toes. She

stopped the machine, then hit the rewind button, not believing her eyes, certain she had to be mistaken.

But there was no mistake. This tape didn't show her grandfather stealing the diamond necklace. It showed Michael Wolff making love to her.

MICHAEL HAD NEVER SEEN Sarah so furious. She burst into the private office he kept on the second floor, the solid oak door banging hard against the wall.

"What the hell is this?" she asked, holding a videotape-cassette adapter in her hand. He recognized the 8mm tape nestled inside.

He rose slowly to his feet, confused by her reaction. "The security tape. I thought you might want it."

She approached his desk, slamming the tape down on top of it. Emerald fire blazed in her eyes. "Want it? As what? A souvenir? A blatant reminder of my stupidity?"

He rounded his desk. "I don't know what you're talking about."

"How about the fact that you lied to me? My grandfather's not on that tape. Instead..." She closed her eyes. "Just please tell me there aren't any copies."

Without a word, Michael picked up the cassette and walked over to the media center in the corner of his office. A moment later, he saw a black and white image of the wall panel concealing the safe in his bedroom.

The date displayed on the screen was December twenty-second. Since each tape held about a week's worth of footage, he hit the fast-forward button on the remote control. But nothing changed on the image until December twenty-eighth, the day that Bertram Hewitt had broken into the safe.

Only the video didn't show the break-in. Because Bertram had obviously figured out the camera was there and had turned the lens in another direction.

Toward the bed.

Three more days flashed by with nothing out of the ordinary. Then the date of December thirty-first appeared on the screen and Michael knew what he was about to see.

The angle of the camera lens was narrow, providing about a five-foot by five-foot view of the round bed. The rest of his bedroom was not visible.

He disengaged the fast-forward button on the remote just in time to watch Sarah, dressed as Little Red Riding Hood, dive into his bed. Then she hastily pulled the heavy canopy drapes closed behind her.

A moment later, he saw his wolf shirt fly through the air. Then his pants. Saw himself walk past wearing nothing more than boxer shorts and knew this must be when he'd used that spear to scratch away that mad itch on his back.

Michael's mouth went dry as he saw himself approach the bed and fling back the canopy drapes. He recalled the erotic surge of pleasure he'd experienced at the moment he'd found her there and felt it shoot through him now.

He saw Sarah's startled expression on the tape, the spark of panic in her green eyes.

Because the security camera recorded video only, no audio, he couldn't hear their conversation. But it made the events of that night so much clearer to him now. Because he could watch her reactions instead of concentrating on her words.

He saw the deep flush on her cheeks as she stared up at him, the tension in her body when he joined her on the bed.

Michael turned away from the television screen for a moment to see Sarah standing beside him now, watching his face.

Her anger had vanished. "You didn't know about the camera being moved?"

He shook his head, speechless, then turned back to the television. He watched himself kissing her now and saw all too clearly what he didn't realize then.

She wasn't kissing him back. Her arms hung stiffly at her sides, her fists clenching the bedsheets as his hands untied the cloak at her throat. She appeared to be barely enduring his caresses.

The image on the television screen brought a bitter

taste to his mouth. Michael had always prided himself on his ability to satisfy a woman, to anticipate her every wish between the sheets. But that night he'd been completely oblivious to anything but his own overwhelming desire for Sarah. "You should have stopped me."

"I know." She moved beside him, her voice almost a whisper. "But I didn't want to stop."

Her words filled him with something he couldn't define. But as he continued to watch the television screen he knew that she'd spoken the truth.

He saw the tension in her body ease as she circled her arms around his neck and finally began kissing him back. Saw her head tip back and her eyelids flutter shut as his mouth moved down the length of her throat. Saw her lick her lips and feather her long, slender fingers over his bare chest.

Michael couldn't wrench his gaze from the images in front of him. His body grew hot and heavy with arousal, all too aware of the woman standing beside him—the woman he was making love to on the television screen. He couldn't let himself look at her now. Couldn't let himself touch her. Not without losing complete control.

He couldn't hide his arousal from her either. It strained prominently against the wool fabric of his black dress pants. His entire body throbbed with it.

Sucking in a deep breath, Michael was suddenly

aware that Sarah wasn't watching the screen any-more. She was watching him.

She turned slowly toward him, then reached out and placed her hand lightly on his belt buckle. Her fingers swept low to brush over the very tip of him.

A groan erupted from his throat and he closed his eyes. But he still didn't move, his body almost shaking now. Michael had let his passion overwhelm him once before. This time it was up to Sarah to lead the way.

She did. Literally. Taking his hand, she led him to his massive mahogany desk. Then she backed him up against it, the hard edge of the wood digging into the base of his spine. But that minor discomfort dissolved when she sank her soft body into him, rising up on her toes to nip his lower lip. Michael gripped the edge of the desk with both hands as she turned her attention to the buttons on his shirt. Slipping each one free as her hips pressed into him. Again and again. The intimate pressure was sweet torture and he feared he wouldn't last long enough to get his pants off.

But Sarah was taking care of that little problem. She tugged his shirttails out of his waistband with urgency, her breathing as unsteady as his own. Then she peeled the shirt off his shoulders, her gaze drinking in the hard muscles of his chest. She leaned forward to flick her tongue over one flat nipple as her fingers worked his belt buckle. Michael knew at that moment he was completely in her power.

Just like he'd been since the moment they'd first made love.

His control over her had been an illusion. A lie he'd been telling himself whenever his need for her had threatened to overwhelm him. But she stripped it all away now, along with the rest of his clothes.

Michael couldn't deny the truth to himself any longer. He needed her. Not just her body, but her mind and heart as well. All of her. Every day. For the rest of his life.

That's what he wanted, but what about her? Did she want him? Just him? Doubt about her true feelings still flickered in some deep, dark, secret place inside of him. Doubts he wanted to drive away. Now. Forever.

While she shed her own clothes, Michael reached behind him and swept the top of his desk clear. Folders and papers crashed to the floor in a chaotic heap. But he didn't care. Nothing mattered to him except holding Sarah in his arms.

Lying back on the desk, he pulled her on top of him, relishing the warmth of her silky, smooth skin and the perfect way the curves of her body melded to his.

"I need you," he whispered against her supple mouth. "Now."

Sarah knew she couldn't go back now. She didn't want to go back, not when she sensed an urgency in him that was more than physical. That almost touched her soul.

Michael lifted her hips and buried himself deep inside her, making her lose all rational thought. They moved together in perfect rhythm—just like the couple on the television screen.

She and Michael found their release at the same moment, their cries blending in primal harmony. As they clung to each other, Sarah realized she'd been guilty of placing the chains of captivity around her own heart.

Now…she was finally free.

THE LONE HOWL of a wolf awoke Sarah and she found herself in the safe haven of Michael's arms. He'd carried her up to his bedroom around midnight and made sweet, slow love to her again.

She glanced at the nightstand and saw the time glowing in bright red numbers. Four o'clock in the morning.

A familiar bark seeped through the bedroom wall and Sarah knew Napoleon was answering the call of the wolf. Three more barks made Michael's eyes flutter open beside her.

"Your mutt is making a racket," he said with a weary groan.

"I know." She leaned closer to kiss the corner of his mouth. "But he's all bark and no bite. Just like you."

Sparks of desire lit his gray eyes as he pulled her close to him. "As I recall, you're the one who likes to bite."

"They're called love nips," she replied, demonstrating this to him by catching his lower lip between her teeth.

A demonstration that turned into a deep, hot kiss.

Napoleon's now frantic barking made them both pull away for air. Michael flopped back against the pillow. "Is he ever going to stop?"

She nestled against him, her head resting on his shoulder. "Why do you hate dogs so much?"

"Kiss me again and I'll tell you."

But Sarah knew a stall when she heard it. If she started kissing him, they wouldn't stop—which wouldn't be bad at all, except she still wouldn't have an answer to her question.

She leaned up on her elbow and looked into his eyes. "Tell me and then I'll kiss you."

He sighed. "I don't hate dogs. I just don't like them in the house. They make me...uncomfortable."

She reached up and slid her palm over his jaw, enjoying the sensation of his rough whiskers on her skin. "So you've never owned a dog?"

He grasped her hand and brought it to his mouth.

"Once," he replied, kissing the tips of each of her fingers. "When I was nine."

His mouth moved to the inside of her wrist, his lips over her pulse point. No doubt he could feel the way he was affecting her heartbeat. His sensuous mouth moved slowly up her arm, but she wasn't about to let him distract her from the subject at hand.

"How long did you keep him?" she asked.

"Eight days."

Eight days? What boy only keeps a dog eight days? Unless something horrible had happened. An accident?

Michael was kissing her shoulder now, his mouth moving to her collarbone, then even lower. Her breasts started to tingle in anticipation.

"Why only eight..." Sarah gasped when his mouth found her nipple. "Oh, Michael..."

Arching her back, she moaned aloud as he worshipped her breast with his tongue, then lavished the same patient attention on her other breast.

She was determined to stay focused. Difficult to do when his hand began sliding up her bare thigh. "Why...only...eight...days?"

"Because I told my grandfather to sell him."

"Mmmm...why?"

His warm sigh caressed the tip of her erect nipple. Then he rolled on top of her, kissing her full on the mouth. "I can't concentrate when you keep asking me questions."

She knew now that her instincts had been right. There was something about her dog that brought back memories he didn't want to share. Memories that explained the pain she now saw in his eyes.

Circling her arms around his neck, she whispered, "I love you, Michael Wolff."

Then she kissed him long and hard and deep, determined to vanquish that pain with the strength of her love for him.

MUCH LATER, when she lay boneless in his arms, Michael answered her question. "I told my grandfather to sell the dog because I couldn't stand the sight of him."

He paused, but Sarah just waited in silence for him to continue in his own time, determined not to pelt him with any more questions.

"I went to camp that summer in North Carolina. It was the first time I'd ever been that far away from home for that long." He threaded his fingers through her hair, softly stroking the strands. "When I came home," he continued, his voice flat and even, "my mother was gone."

She tilted her head up to look at him, a question on the tip of her tongue. But she held back. This was his story and she wanted him to tell it his way.

"Nobody told me my parents were getting a divorce, so I didn't believe my dad when he kept telling me she wasn't here. I looked in every room. Over and over again."

Her throat tightened as she nestled her cheek against his chest.

"And the whole time," Michael said, "there was this dog chasing after me, tugging at my pant cuffs and chasing after my shoelaces, getting in the way of my search."

All the pieces started to fit together now. She closed her eyes, finally understanding why he couldn't seem to stand the sight of Napoleon. Her dog, any dog, was a visible reminder of his mother's abandonment.

"She didn't even say goodbye," Michael whispered, as if it still shocked him after all these years. "Just took the hefty divorce settlement my father had promised her if she didn't fight for custody and left.

"That's why I didn't want the dog," he continued. "I didn't want to love anything that could run away from me again."

Tears stung her eyes. She finally understood the reason he suspected Blair was behind his grandfather's accidents. Why he thought the Wolff family was jinxed. Why he thought money could buy anything—except love.

She licked her lips, still slightly swollen from his kisses. "I don't know what to say."

"Say you'll stay." He pulled her close against his big, warm body. "Napoleon can even live here with us—bark his head off if he wants. I have you now, Sarah. I don't need anything or anyone else."

Neither did she. But Sarah feared a future with Michael Wolff could only hold heartache. Those lingering doubts would always be with him, thanks to the legacy left to him by his mother. Despite his feelings for her, some small part of him would always wonder if Sarah found the Wolff fortune his most attractive feature.

She couldn't stand the thought of those doubts clouding their love until it withered and died. But she only knew one way to stop that from happening.

So she didn't say anything at all.

14

THE NEXT MORNING all hell broke loose.

Michael awoke to the sound of someone pounding hard on his bedroom door. He stood up and grabbed his robe, cinching it around his nude body.

Sarah rose up on her elbows, her hair tumbling around her bare shoulders. "What's going on?"

He knew in that moment that he'd never get tired of waking up with her. "That's what I intend to find out. Stay here."

Closing the canopy drapes around his bed to conceal her presence, he stalked toward the door, ready to tear somebody's head off.

Only when he opened it, he changed his mind. Assaulting a police office was not a good idea.

"Michael Wolff?" the cop asked him.

"Yes." He saw other police officers in the hallway now and heard the squawk of their radios.

The cop moved out of the doorway. "Would you step out here, please? I'd like to ask you a few questions."

"What questions?" he asked, walking into the hallway. "What the hell is going on here?"

Blair appeared in the doorway of the room she shared with his grandfather, her blue eyes wide in her pale face. "Seamus is missing."

Michael looked at the cop, then back at Blair again. "Missing? What do you mean?"

"I mean he's not here, not anywhere." Her shrill voice cut through the last of his cobwebs. Michael was fully awake now.

"He left the house?"

Blair shook her head. "All the cars are still here. So is his wallet. He can't get far enough with his cane to walk anywhere."

"So you called the police? Why didn't you wake me up first?" Michael demanded.

She lifted her chin. "Because we're not going to let your so-called investigator solve the crime this time."

"This time?" the cop echoed, turning to Blair. "Was there a previous incident I should know about?"

"No," Michael said.

"Yes," Blair countered, then faced the officer. "Two weeks ago, someone broke into my husband's safe. The only copy of his most recent will was stolen and hasn't been recovered yet."

The cop pulled out a notepad. "Did you report this break-in?"

Blair's mouth thinned. "Michael convinced my

husband not to call the police. He promised to handle it himself. And now...Seamus is missing."

Michael couldn't believe she was implicating him in the disappearance of his grandfather.

The cop jotted down some more notes. "May I ask who is the main beneficiary of this new will?"

"I am," Blair replied. "He left me his entire estate."

The cop turned to him. "You were excluded?"

"I don't need or want his money," Michael replied. "Look, this is crazy. My grandfather was safe in his bed last night. I know because I was the last one who saw him."

That went in the cop's notebook too, and Michael sensed it had been the wrong thing to say.

He turned toward the stairs, ready to start looking for Seamus himself. "He's got to be around here somewhere."

But the cop stepped into his path. "We're already conducting a thorough search of the premises, sir. We'd like to include your room in that search if you don't have any objections."

He hesitated, thinking about Sarah naked in his bed. "Of course not. If you'll just give a moment..."

The cop's antennae shot up at that. "We'd prefer you to remain with us at all times, sir—for your own safety."

Michael knew that wasn't the reason, but before he could reply, Sarah stepped out of his bedroom.

She wore the same clothes she'd had on yesterday, though noticeably wrinkled now. She'd been unable to tame her hair and her slender feet were bare, since they'd both left their shoes in his office last night.

Her worried gaze went straight to Michael. "What's wrong?"

"Blair thinks Seamus has been kidnapped," he explained. "Will you please tell the cops that my grandfather is perfectly able to get around by himself now? He's probably just wandering in the house somewhere."

"Seamus is almost fully recovered," she said, turning to the cop. "I've been taking care of him for the past few weeks."

The cop looked from Sarah to Michael's bedroom and back again. "May I ask who hired you?"

"I did," Michael said through clenched teeth.

That went in the cop's notes, too. Then he waved a few of his fellow officers into Michael's room.

When Michael tried to follow them, the cop stopped him. "If you'll just wait out here, sir, we need to conduct interviews with everyone in the house."

But Michael knew he was already a suspect in their eyes. As soon as they found Seamus's will in his room, they'd be able to pin a motive on him.

It only took them ten minutes.

SARAH STOOD ALONE in the Denver police station, too worried about Michael and Seamus to pay much attention to the early morning chaos around her. The strong aroma of coffee filled the air and several telephones rang at once.

The detectives had taken Michael in for questioning almost three hours ago. Sarah hadn't been able to ride into the city with him because the police were adamant about interviewing her, along with the rest of the staff.

She'd watched enough episodes of *Law & Order* to know her rights. So when they'd begun asking her about the stolen will and her personal relationship with Michael, she'd simply refused to answer any more questions.

Since they had no evidence against her, they had no choice but to let her go. That's when she'd headed straight to the police station. To Michael.

After what seemed an eternity, he finally emerged from the interview room, looking haggard and tired. His lawyer was walking beside him and she recognized him as one of the guests from the dinner party.

"I'll be in touch, Michael," the lawyer said, with a nod toward Sarah. Then he walked out the door.

"Are you all right?" she asked him, moving in close.

"Yes." He kissed her, then grasped her elbow, steering her toward the exit. "Let's get out of here."

Only they found even more chaos outside the police station. Reporters shouted questions at them as they walked down the steps, shoving microphones in their faces.

"Mr. Wolff, do the police plan to file charges against you for kidnapping?"

"Is it true you need his estate to save your business empire, Mr. Wolff?"

"Do you believe your grandfather, Seamus Wolff, is still alive?"

Sarah winced at the bright lights of the television cameras, then grabbed Michael's hand in her own. Half running now, she led him to her Toyota, both of them quickly ducking inside.

She jammed her key into the ignition, shifted into gear, then floored it as she pulled away from the curb, leaving the reporters behind on the sidewalk.

Michael turned to her. "What the hell is happening?"

"Apparently, the call about Seamus's disappearance went out over the police scanner and reporters picked it up. When they showed up at the mansion, Blair gave interviews."

"And no doubt made me look guilty as hell."

"I'm afraid so." She turned off onto a quiet street, then parked under an oak tree before plunging into his arms. They just held each other for a long time, not saying anything at all.

But Sarah knew she had to find a way to help him. "Do you think Blair's behind Seamus's disappearance?"

He rested his cheek on the top of her head. "I don't know what to think anymore. The police are just itching to arrest me, but my attorney told me not to answer any questions."

"Good advice," she agreed. "So they don't know why the will was in your room?"

He met her gaze. "No. And I don't plan to tell them how it got there either."

"But maybe if we just explain…"

He shook his head. "I won't let you be implicated, Sarah. I'll make a full confession myself before that happens. It will be your word against mine."

A month ago she'd said the exact same thing to him, only then she'd said it to protect her grandfather. Now Michael was saying it to protect her.

His warm breath feathered her hair. "Maybe you should go home."

"My home is with you." As she said the words, she knew they were true. Last night she'd been afraid of a future with him. But she couldn't live her life in fear. If some part of Michael believed she loved him for his money, then she'd just have to find a way to prove him wrong.

Michael pulled away far enough to look into her

face. "My home might be a Colorado state prison if I'm charged with kidnapping. Or worse."

"You didn't kidnap Seamus," she cried. "I was with you all night long. I can give you an alibi."

"Blair already believes we're in collusion. No doubt the police will think the same."

But she wasn't willing to give up so easily. "There has to be something we can do."

"Let's go home," he said wearily. "Before the reporters catch up with us."

Sarah nodded, pulling out onto the street. At least he wasn't playing noble and trying to kick her out of his life again.

And, anyway, she wouldn't let him. Unlike his mother, she wasn't going anywhere.

THAT EVENING, there still had been no word about Seamus. Michael had mixed feelings when the police finally cleared out. On the one hand, he was glad to be out from their unceasing observation. On the other, he felt as if they had given up on his grandfather ever returning home safely.

Blair had left, too, refusing to stay in the same house as Michael. With only he and Sarah left in the huge mansion, Michael had let all the servants go home early.

Then he'd let Sarah take him to bed. Not that he'd put up much of a fight. For a very short, very sweet time, Michael had been able to forget about everything except the joy of being in her arms. But, unlike Sarah, he'd been unable to fall asleep afterward. So he'd left her upstairs in his bed and returned to the first-floor parlor to stare out the huge window.

The light of the moon reflected off the snow and he could hear a wolf howl in the distance. Was his grandfather out in the cold night somewhere?

None of this made sense. There'd been no sign of forced entry into the house, no sign of a struggle. The only possible warning that something was wrong last night was Napoleon's frantic barking.

Had the dog been trying to warn them?

He clenched his jaw, wanting answers but always coming up with more questions. The only thing he knew for certain was that he wouldn't let Sarah get hurt, no matter what he had to do.

Napoleon walked into the room, his toenails clicking on the hardwood floor.

"Hey, mutt," Michael murmured, turning his gaze back to the window. Had something just moved out there?

He took a step closer, straining to see in the darkness. There it was again. His pulse picked up when he saw an old man slowly emerging from behind a stand of pine trees.

His grandfather?

Michael rushed to the foyer, unlocking the door

and swinging it open just as the man mounted the steps.

Only it wasn't Seamus.

Michael stared into the brown eyes of a stranger, his disappointment bringing a bitter taste to his mouth. "Who are you?"

"Where is she?" the old man barked, answering Michael's question with one of his own. "Where's my Sarah?"

He stepped aside to let the old man in. "You must be Bertram Hewitt."

"What have you done to her?" he demanded, looking into the foyer as if expecting to find her chained to a wall. His wrinkled face was bright red from the cold. Icy shards of snow clung to his pants all the way up to his knees.

"Get in here before you freeze to death," Michael ordered.

"I wouldn't give Seamus Wolff the satisfaction of freezing on his front stoop," Bertram replied, stepping inside. "I'm here for my granddaughter, so don't even think about trying to stop me. I didn't let that locked gate out there hold me back and I'm sure as hell not afraid to take you on, either."

Michael could see the furious determination in the man's eyes, so he simply nodded. "Go ahead. I love your granddaughter too much to try and stop you."

Bertram blanched. "Love her? That's not possible."

A month ago he would have agreed with him. But Sarah had found her way into his heart. He didn't even care anymore if his fortune had helped soften her toward him. Hell, he'd even be grateful. Because he couldn't imagine his life now without Sarah in it.

"If you've laid one hand on her..." Bertram muttered, brushing past him.

"Sarah is fine."

The old man whirled on him, lean and surprisingly agile for his age. "She sure didn't look fine when I saw her on the six o'clock news, standing outside a police station!"

"She was there for me," he explained. "My grandfather is missing and..."

"Yeah," Bertram interjected, "that's the only good news I've heard all day."

His words made Michael's fists clench. Sarah wanted to protect this guy?

Then he thought of his own cantankerous grandfather and realized that you couldn't pick your family. All you could do was love them and put up with them and trust that everything would come out all right.

It was a trust that was quickly beginning to ebb for Michael. His grandfather had been missing for almost twelve hours. There had been no leads. No ransom note. No...body.

"I'll ask you again," Bertram said, tugging off his gloves, oblivious to the rather large, muddy puddle he was making on the floor as the snow dripped off of him. "Where is Sarah?"

"She's upstairs." Michael moved toward the staircase. "Third floor. I'll take you to her."

"Don't bother." Bertram brushed past him again, then turned and wagged a finger in the air. "I let a Wolff hurt one woman I loved. I swear on my wife's grave I won't let it happen to another."

Michael watched him vault up the stairs, leaving a trail of snow and mud and pine needles in his wake. Could Bertram convince Sarah to go home with him? Could she stop him, even if she wanted to?

Michael mounted the steps to the second floor, taking care to avoid Bertram's muddy footprints. Then he turned toward his office. This was between Sarah and her grandfather—a man who obviously loved Sarah as much as he did.

Michael sat at his desk, too distracted to work. So he stared at the phone instead, waiting for the police to call and tell him they'd found his grandfather. Then he stared at the door, waiting for Sarah to tell him she was leaving him. But the door stayed firmly closed.

His gaze strayed to the media center. That security

tape was still inside the videocassette recorder. He walked over and ejected the tape, turning it over in his hands. Then he inserted it back into the machine and hit the erase button. If his lawyer was correct and Seamus didn't show up in the next twenty-four hours, Michael could be arrested. And Sarah could possibly be named as his co-conspirator.

No matter what happened, he didn't want any attorney or judge or jury watching that tape, tainting the special night that had brought them together.

A night he could never erase from his heart.

BERTRAM HEWITT couldn't find his granddaughter anywhere. No doubt Seamus's grandson had lied to him, a skill the Wolff family seemed to come by naturally. He abandoned the third floor, taking a back staircase. He knew every nook and cranny of this sprawling mansion, having had plenty of time to memorize the blueprints in prison.

Just like that newscast tonight would be forever burned on his brain. At first, he hadn't recognized his own granddaughter. Hadn't wanted to believe it was really her. But the distress on her face had gone straight to his heart. His little Sarah needed help.

And he damn well wasn't going to stop until he found her.

Could the Wolffs be holding her prisoner? Keeping her somewhere against her will? It was the only thing that made sense. He'd taught her to hate the Wolff name since she could speak her first word. She'd never come here of her own volition.

Was Seamus making him pay for stealing that necklace? Or for stealing the woman he loved fifty years ago?

It seemed to Bertram as if it had all happened yesterday instead of five decades ago. Anna's tearful confession that she'd let Seamus kiss her. The fistfight between he and Wolff that she never knew about. That's when they both knew they couldn't stay in business together anymore.

Seamus had taken that diamond necklace with him as a parting cheap shot, severing their friendship forever. Sometimes it still hurt, even after all this time.

Bertram looked around the long hallway, wondering where he should start to look. If only Sarah knew he was here searching for her she could bang on a door or send him some kind of signal.

Then it hit him.

He slowly turned around, staring at the end of the hallway. There was one room where no one would hear her, no matter how loud she screamed or cried out for help. One room that few people knew about, because there was no door. At least, not one you could see.

Could the Wolffs be keeping her there?

Bertram shot down the hallway, his knees trembling. But when he reached the wall he didn't stop. He pushed aside the panel and stepped inside the secret room. But he didn't find his granddaughter there.

He found Seamus Wolff.

15

SARAH FINALLY FOUND Michael in his office, his head resting on his arms atop the desk and Napoleon curled around his feet. She set down the dinner tray she was carrying and just looked at him, his face relaxed in slumber with one lock of his dark hair spilling over his forehead. When she brushed it back with her fingertips, he opened his eyes.

"You're still here."

She smiled at the surprise in his voice. "Where else would I be?"

He sat up. "The way your grandfather barged into the house, I figured you'd be long gone by now."

She blinked. "My grandfather?"

He pushed his chair back and rose to his feet. "Didn't he find you?"

"No," she replied, wondering if he'd been dreaming. "I've been in the kitchen, making us some homemade chicken noodle soup."

She'd worked hard to get the noodles just right, throwing out the first batch of dough. Her grandmother had taught her to cook and had been just as finicky about her noodles.

But Michael didn't even look at the two steaming bowls on the tray. He glanced down at his watch. "The last time I saw Bertram was over two hours ago."

"What exactly was he doing here?"

"He came for you. Apparently, we were featured on the six o'clock news."

She closed her eyes. "Oh, no."

"Oh, yes."

"Did you tell him why I was here?"

Michael shook his head. "Since he was already on the verge of punching me out, I thought I should leave that up to you."

"Punching you out?"

"He's convinced I'm keeping you here against your will."

She rounded the desk, cupping his handsome face in her hands, then leaning down to kiss him. "Not anymore."

His hands circled her waist. "In case I haven't mentioned it, I'm glad you're here. But your grandfather doesn't feel the same way. I know he wouldn't have left this house without you."

"Then let's go find him," she said, grabbing his hand, "and tell him the family feud is over."

Michael wasn't sure where to start looking—until he saw the large muddy footprints on the marble floor. "Looks like he left us a trail."

They followed it up to the third floor, past the line of family bedrooms, all the way to the end of the hall.

Then the footprints just stopped. As if he'd walked smack into the wall.

"I don't understand," Sarah said, looking up at Michael. "Where did he go from here?"

There was only one place that made any sense, a place Michael hadn't thought about in years, though he'd been fascinated by it as a boy. The original owner had built it as a panic room, a place to hide the family if someone tried to break in—a common practice among wealthy people after the Lindbergh kidnapping.

Michael reached out and pushed on the panel. A hidden door popped open and he saw Sarah's eyes widen in surprise. Then he saw the reason why.

Inside the room, Seamus Wolff and Bertram Hewitt sat side by side, an open bottle of whiskey beside them.

"Rescued at last," Seamus slurred, rising awkwardly to his feet. "Don't let that door shut behind ya, boy, or we'll all be trapped in here for eternity." He slanted a glance toward Bertram. "That's my idea of hell."

"Grandpa," Sarah said, rushing to Bertram's side, "are you all right?"

"Never better," he replied, reaching for the whiskey bottle and missing. He tipped it over, the amber liquid spilling onto the concrete floor. "Whoops."

"There should be more somewhere in this place," Seamus said, then turned and fell into his grandson's arms. "Pardon me."

Michael just held him tight for a long moment. "I'm so glad you're all right."

"All right?" Seamus cried, reeling back in surprise. "How can you say that? Don't you know we spilled the whiskey?"

He smiled. "I think you've had enough whiskey. It's time to pour you into bed."

Seamus turned unsteadily to Bertram. "That's why I have to come in here to drink. This boy's always trying to tell me what to do."

Michael's eyes widened. "You mean you came in here voluntarily?"

"Hell, yes," Seamus exclaimed. "It's the only place a man can get any peace around here. What with barking dogs and people running up and down the hallway all night long."

Then Seamus's gaze narrowed on Sarah and he pointed an unsteady finger at her. "Did you know this woman is a Hewitt?"

"Yeah," Michael replied, his gaze softening on her. "I know."

"Does this mean you two have actually been talking?" Sarah asked.

"Not much else to do," Bertram explained.

Seamus nodded. "I've been stuck in here since late last night. Then Bertram walks in and I was all ready to offer him a reward for rescuing me, until he let the damn door close behind him."

"Then we were both trapped," Bertram finished.

Sarah looked at the two of them. "Sounds like it was a good opportunity to work out your differences."

"Hell, no," Bertram countered. "I still plan to beat the crap out of him. But not while he's using that cane. It would be too easy."

Seamus took a menacing, if wobbly, step toward his old nemesis. "We'll just see about that."

But Michael held him back. "I think we should continue this discussion in the morning."

"Good idea," Sarah said, helping her grandfather to his feet. "I'll drive him home."

"It's late," Michael said. "And he's in no condition to walk much farther than the nearest bed. He can sleep in one of the spare rooms tonight."

"Under the same roof as a Wolff?" Bertram cried. "Never!" Then his knees buckled and he hit the floor, his head lolling to one side.

"That man never could hold his liquor," Seamus said, tilting precariously on his feet.

Michael grabbed his grandfather's arm and hoisted it around his shoulders. Then he glanced back at Sarah. "I'll be back for your grandfather after I tuck mine into bed."

She nodded, grateful that Seamus and Bertram hadn't tried to kill each other while they were trapped together in here. But judging from their near brawl just now, the feud was still going strong.

At least Bertram hadn't tried to tear her away from the man she loved. Or worse, made her choose between them. That bottle of whiskey had given them all a reprieve. For tonight, anyway.

But what about tomorrow?

THE NEXT AFTERNOON, the four of them sat in the library. The Hewitts were seated in wing chairs on one side of the Persian rug, the Wolffs on the other. Napoleon the dog lay curled asleep in the middle, so Michael wasn't sure which side of the battle he was on.

Seamus and Bertram both sported hangovers today, but they still had enough energy to glower at each other.

Michael loved his grandfather and he knew how much Sarah loved hers. They'd both gone to extremes to protect them. Maybe that was their mistake. Maybe it was time to stop protecting them.

Michael stood up, his gaze moving from Seamus to Bertram. "I think it's time you two learned how Sarah and I met."

Seamus snorted. "I'd rather hear why she's been masquerading as my caretaker. Probably spying for Bertram."

Bertram rose half out of his chair. "My grand-daughter's no spy. I didn't need a spy to steal that necklace from you. Twice!"

Seamus scowled. "Twice? What the hell are you talking about? Do we need to frisk you before you leave? Which can't be soon enough for me, by the way!"

Sarah held up both hands. "Hold it, you two. Michael and I are willing to answer all your questions, but if you're not even willing to listen, then what's the point?"

That shut them both up, temporarily anyway.

Seamus settled back into his chair. "Go ahead."

Michael waited for Bertram to resume his seat before he spoke. "It all started at the masquerade ball on New Year's Eve."

"I crashed the New Year's Eve party," Sarah interjected, "dressed as Little Red Riding Hood." She smiled at Michael. "And I attracted the attention of a wolf."

The woman still had his attention, her smile going straight to his heart.

"We danced," Michael told them. "And I asked her to meet me at midnight for the unmasking."

"Only I already had another appointment," Sarah

shifted in her chair, "to break into the master safe and return the diamond necklace my grandfather had stolen the week before."

Bertram stared at her in disbelief. "Return it? That necklace is your legacy."

Her gaze softened on him. "I had to do it, Grandpa. I couldn't let you go back to prison."

"Only I caught her in the act," Michael said, skipping over the incredible night they'd spent in his bed. There were some things their family didn't need to know.

"He thought I was stealing the necklace," Sarah explained. "When I told him the truth and begged him not to turn me or my grandfather over to the police, he offered me a deal."

Seamus leaned back in his chair and folded his arms across his chest. "I can't wait to hear this."

Bertram snorted. "I'm still waiting to hear why my granddaughter would give up a necklace that rightfully belongs to her."

"Be quiet and let them finish," Seamus admonished, his gaze now fixed on his grandson. "Keep talking."

Michael took a deep breath. "I blackmailed Sarah into hiring on as your caretaker so she could break into your private safe and steal your will for me."

"Steal my will..." Seamus gaped at him. "Why?"

"Because I thought Blair was responsible for your

accidents. The timing of them, since you'd just made her your sole beneficiary, seemed more than coincidental. I even had her investigated, certain she was trying to kill you."

Seamus heaved a deep sigh. "Damn."

Bertram turned to Sarah. "Let me get this straight. You let this man blackmail you...to protect me?"

"She was ready to go to prison in your place," Michael informed him.

Bertram blanched, the righteous indignation draining out of him. "Damn."

Michael turned back to his grandfather. "Just so we're clear, I'm completely responsible for the theft of your will. Sarah didn't want to do it, but I left her no choice."

"There's something I think you should know, Michael," Seamus announced, looking a little sheepish. "Blair didn't arrange those accidents. I did." Then he rubbed his hip. "Though that last one went too far."

"You cut the brake line on the car?" Michael asked, not certain he was hearing right. "You purposely fell down the stairs?"

Seamus gave a stiff nod. "Stupid, I know. But not as stupid as a seventy-year-old man wanting to keep proving to himself that his thirty-four-year-old wife really loves him. I arranged those 'accidents' to see if she really cares."

"Damn," Bertram said again, staring at Seamus.

"The truth is that she doesn't love me," Seamus admitted. "Not the way a man wants to be loved." His gaze settled on Bertram. "Not the way Anna loved you."

Bertram cleared his throat. "Did you mean what you told me last night or was that just the whiskey talking?"

Seamus shook his head. "If I'd known Anna was sick, I would have given away everything I owned to save her. I swear it."

Michael looked at Sarah and saw the tears gleaming in her eyes. It might not be a declaration of peace, exactly, but it was a beginning.

Then he turned back to his grandfather. "I guess I owe your wife an apology."

"So do I," Seamus replied. "I knew when Blair married me that she didn't really love me. But she needed me. Needed the money and security I could give her. Only unlike you, Michael, I was too much of a coward to find out why."

"She had her reasons," Sarah interjected. "I really don't think she's a bad person."

"I agree." Seamus reached for his cane, then rose to his feet. "That's why I'm going to let her go, but with enough money to provide her with whatever she needs for the rest of her life."

"Before you leave, Seamus," Sarah said, "I have a confession of my own to make. I'm the one who took my grandmother's letter out of your safe. I know I had no right to invade your privacy, but I wanted to read it and see if I could finally understand this feud between you."

"A feud that's ending today," Michael announced. He walked over to stand beside her chair. "I love Sarah and we're going to be together."

Too late he realized how dictatorial he sounded. Sarah wasn't his prisoner anymore. She was free to make her own choice—even if that choice wasn't him.

Michael cleared his throat. "If she wants me."

For a long moment she didn't move and Michael's heart froze in his chest. Then she was in his arms.

"I want you," she announced, thawing the icy emptiness inside of him. "I love you, Michael Wolff. Now and always."

Then she kissed him, long and deep, until the sound of Bertram clearing his throat made them break apart. Michael could feel Sarah tense in his arms as they both turned to watch Bertram rise slowly to his feet, his expression grave.

"I love my granddaughter more than anything in this world. If you make her happy..." Bertram paused to take a deep breath before extending his hand, "then I won't stand in your way."

Michael shook the old man's hand, surprised by the firmness of his grip.

"Neither will I," Seamus announced, pulling a familiar blue velvet case out of his pocket, "and neither will this."

No one moved or spoke.

"Fifty years ago," Seamus said, "I cheated my business partner because a woman had broken my heart."

He limped over to stand beside Sarah. "I used this necklace to get rich so I could prove to Anna that she'd chosen the wrong man. But when I see how much my grandson loves you, I know it all worked out for the best."

He lifted the lid, the diamonds sparkling in the light. "This necklace belongs to you now, Sarah. Your grandfather is right—this is your legacy."

Then he placed it around her neck, struggling with the difficult clasp.

"Let me," Michael offered.

Seamus stepped aside and let his grandson fasten the necklace around her neck.

"Perfect," Bertram breathed as he stared at his granddaughter.

Seamus nodded. "She's as beautiful as Anna, both inside and out."

"If you're lucky," Bertram said, "someday she may be your granddaughter-in-law."

Seamus smiled. "I'd be proud to have her become a Wolff."

"How do you know she won't keep the name Hewitt?" Bertram retorted. "Lots of married women these days prefer to use their maiden name."

Seamus moved toward the door. "Hold that argument until I get rid of this damn headache. I've got a great hangover cure in the kitchen if you care to join me."

Bertram followed him. "It's that rotgut whiskey you drink. A person would think a man with your kind of money could afford the good stuff."

"You wouldn't know good whiskey if it bit you on the behind," Seamus quipped. "Remember that stuff you brewed after we built that still? It could eat through concrete."

"Then you must have one tough stomach since you drank away most of our profits." Then Bertram laughed. "Remember the time you added too much corn mash?"

"Me? That was your fault...."

Their voices trailed off as they disappeared down the hallway.

"Amazing," Sarah said, stepping into Michael's arms. "They're actually still speaking to us—and to each other."

He pulled her close. "Sounds more like arguing to me. Now where can we go for some peace and quiet? Paris? Venice? Vienna?" He leaned down to brush her lips with his own. "How about all three?"

She pressed her body against him. "How about the secret room upstairs?"

"Good idea," he said, kissing her again. "I had the door fixed this morning so it can only be locked from the inside now."

"Sounds like a good safety precaution."

"And I'm the only one with a key. I intend to make it my own private lair."

Sarah smiled as he rocked his hips against her. "My, what big...*plans* you have, Mr. Wolff."

"Absolutely." He gave her a predatory grin, then scooped her up in his arms. "This is one story that's going to end happily ever after."

_____Epilogue_____

One year later

MICHAEL STOOD outside the private dining room in the Palace Arms, one of his favorite restaurants in the trendy LoDo section of downtown Denver, holding his cell phone to his ear. He knew Sarah was waiting for him inside, but he had to get rid of his lawyer first.

"Yes, I understand the possible consequences," Michael said. "And the answer is still no." Then he disconnected the line and snapped his cell phone closed.

Ever since Michael and Sarah had announced their engagement five months ago, his lawyers had been hounding him to make her sign a prenuptial agreement. They'd even taken the liberty of drawing up a draft copy for his perusal.

Michael hadn't bothered to read it before tearing it up. He knew a prenuptial agreement made good business sense. Knew about the Wolffs' dismal matrimonial track record. Knew if Sarah truly loved him, then signing a prenuptial agreement shouldn't matter to her.

But it mattered to him.

As far as Michael was concerned, everything he owned already belonged to Sarah, including his heart. So he wasn't about to start their marriage with a contingency plan. He wanted Sarah, no matter what. If he discovered someday that she'd found his fortune his most attractive feature...then he'd just learn to live with it. But in his heart, he had no doubt she loved him for who he was, not what he had.

Michael walked through the door of the private dining room.

Sarah rose from her chair when she saw him. "Hello, gorgeous," she murmured.

As always, just the sight of her filled him with warmth and love. Sarah still took his breath away. She wore the same white gown that she'd worn on his birthday, as well as the diamond necklace that had brought them together.

She'd promised to wear the necklace for the wedding, too, which was still four long weeks away. Seamus and Bertram were in charge of the reception, where they were planning to debut their new line of Hewitt & Wolff Whiskey. Business partners and friends once more, they were determined to make Hewitt & Wolff Distilleries famous.

Michael walked over and kissed his fiancée, then pulled out her chair for her and slid it under her as she sat. "You're looking rather delicious yourself. Can I have you for dessert?"

"Every night," she promised, as he leaned down to nibble the side of her neck. "But no snacking. We have some business to settle first."

That's when Michael noticed the manila envelope on the table in front of her. He watched as she pulled a sheaf of papers from it. "What's that?"

"A prenuptial agreement." She handed it to him. "I'd like you to sign it."

He blinked. She was making *him* sign a prenup? "I don't understand."

"It says you agree to give up your fortune when we marry."

He gaped at her. "Give up my fortune?"

She stood up to face him. "I don't want you for your money, Michael. But there's no way I can ever really prove that to you. So I thought, what if we could start from scratch? What if we could build our own fortune—together?"

The idea strangely appealed to him, but this was crazy. Give away *all* his money? "I don't think you know what you're asking of me, Sarah. Do you have any idea what I'm worth?"

"You're priceless to me," she said softly. "I want *you*, Michael, not your fortune. Since you've been searching for a good foundation to leave your estate, why not start one of your own? Give all your money to it now instead of sixty years from now."

His head was racing. So was his heart. "Start my own foundation?"

"Why not?" She smiled. "You're a wonderful businessman. A foundation would thrive under your direction." Her smile widened. "As the executive director, you could even set your own salary."

"I could do that?"

"You're Michael Wolff," she said, love shining in her green eyes. "You can do anything."

He stared down at the prenuptial agreement, his mind already brimming with possibilities for his foundation. Then he pulled a pen out of his lapel pocket and signed his name with a flourish. Giving up his fortune was easier than he ever imagined.

Almost as easy as loving Sarah. He knew without a shadow of a doubt now that she loved him. *Just him.*

And he felt like the richest man in the world.

They're strong, they're sexy, they're not afraid to use the assets Mother Nature gave them....

Venus Messina is...

#916 WICKED & WILLING
by Leslie Kelly
February 2003

Sydney Colburn is...

#920 BRAZEN & BURNING
by Julie Elizabeth Leto
March 2003

Nicole Bennett is...

#924 RED-HOT & RECKLESS
by Tori Carrington
April 2003

The Bad Girls Club...where membership has its privileges!

Available wherever

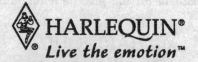

is sold....

HARLEQUIN®
Live the emotion™

Visit us at www.eHarlequin.com

HTBGIRLS

When Suzanne, Nicole and Taylor vow to stay
single, they don't count on meeting these sexy
bachelors!

ROUGHING IT WITH RYAN
January 2003

TANGLING WITH TY
February 2003

MESSING WITH MAC
March 2003

Don't miss this sexy new miniseries by Jill Shalvis—
one of Temptation's hottest authors!

Available at your favorite retail outlet.

Makes any time special ®

Visit us at www.eHarlequin.com

HTSVS

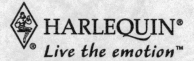

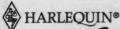

HARLEQUIN®

Temptation

COMING NEXT MONTH

#913 LIGHTNING STRIKES Colleen Collins
The Wrong Bed

The chances of Blaine Saunders's beautiful brass bed being delivered to the wrong address *twice* are about the same as lightning striking twice. Even more surprising, while searching for her missing bed, she ends up in the wrong bed with the right man—the very sexy Donovan Roy! Sparks fly between them, leaving her to wonder if lightning will strike three times....

#914 TANGLING WITH TY Jill Shalvis
South Village Singles #2

Nicole Mann has no time for romance so she's vowed to remain single. No problem. So what's she to do with the too-charming-for-his-own-good Ty O'Grady? Especially because the man won't take no for an answer. Fine. She'll seduce him and get him out of her system...or is it get her out of his system? He has her so confused she hardly knows what day it is! One thing is for sure, *this* is temporary. Or so she thinks....

#915 HOT OFF THE PRESS Nancy Warren

Tess Elliot is just itching for the chance to prove herself as a serious reporter. All she needs is a juicy story. So when the perfect story practically falls in her lap, Tess is all over it. But rival reporter and resident bad boy Mike Grundel wants in on the action, too. Of course, Mike isn't only interested in reporting...getting under Tess's skin is just as much fun. But it's getting her under the covers that's going to take some work!

#916 WICKED & WILLING Leslie Kelly
The Bad Girls Club

Businessman Troy Langtree is making some changes. After his latest fling ended in disaster, he decided to start over—in a new city, in a new job. He's hoping he'll be able to focus on what he wants. Only, once he sees bad girl Venus Messina sunning herself on the balcony, all he wants is *her*. After all, every man knows that bad girls are better....

HTCNM0103